DARREN COLEMAN

Author of *Before I Let Go & Do Or Die*

PRESENTS:

Get LOW

a novel by ®

Nvision Publishing and the above portrayal of a boy looking to the moon and the stars are trademarks of **Nvision incorporated.**

Get Low is an Nvision Book
Nvision Publishing
an imprint of **Power Play Media®**
P. O. box 274, Lanham Severn road, Lanham, MD 20703

This novel is a work of fiction. Any references to real people, events, establishments, or locales are intended only to give the fiction a sense of reality and authenticity. Other names, characters, and incidents occurring in the work are either the product of the author's imagination or are used fictitiously, as are those fictionalized events and incidents that involve real persons. Any character that happens to share the name of a person who is an acquaintance of the author, past or present, is purely coincidental and is in no way intended to be an actual account involving that person.

Book and Cover design by Darren Coleman
Cover Model: Dara Williams
Cover Photography: Taylor Whitehead
Rear Cover Model: Soncerae Smith

Library of Congress Cataloging-in-Publication Data;

D, A novel by
Get Low: a novel by D
    For complete Library of Congress Copyright info visit the nvision publishing web site.

ISBN-13 978-1-934230-01-05
Copyright © 2007

Get Low

a novel by D.®

Acknowledgements

I want to thank each and every dedicated reader who goes out and spends their money on my books. I hear so much positive feedback from those who've proven to be true fans and supporters of my work that I want you to believe that you are the reason why I write and re-write until I'm sure its' worthy of your hard earned dollars.

Second, I would like to thank my test readers Enid Pinner, Andria Lawson, Kamala Mayo and Yolanda Johnson. Special thanks to my editors, Derek Lowe and Giselle Hendy.

I couldn't keep my sanity without my partner Azarel. You are truly one of a kind, a diamond in an industry and world full of CZ's.

I'm wishing much continued success for Danette Majette, J. Tremble, Tonia Ridley and everyone at Life Changing Books/Powerplay Media. And for Joy King – the Bonnie to my Clyde, I'm hoping all your dreams come true *all the time.*

Check me out at www.myspace.com/darrencolemanbooks and let me know how you enjoyed the book.

Love to one and all who got love for me.

...*and* Make a Wish

Chapter One

On my fifteenth birthday my family threw a cookout at my Uncle Wade and Aunt Valerie's house that was just as much a party for them as it was for me. Even though I was too old to have a traditional birthday party, my father still dropped sixty bucks and bought me a huge, sheet cake from the Rolling Pin, my favorite bakery, which happened to have the best cakes for miles. Somewhere amongst the crabs, burgers, chicken and alcoholic beverages, my aunt promised that we'd find the time to blow out my candles and cut the cake.

My Aunt Valerie, who was my mother's twin, was smart as hell. She married a generous man with plenty of money. Uncle Wade, along with his partner, Dean, owned about twenty moving trucks and was ultra-successful. They lived in Accokeek, Maryland, which was only fifteen minutes away from our home in Southeast, Washington, D.C. Still, the immaculately kept lawns, estate-sized homes and fancy cars, made it seem like another world. I really didn't care about that though. I was excited because it was the middle of summer, July 15th to be exact, and they had a huge backyard with a pool, a basketball court and a dock since their home backed to the Potomac River.

The day had been incredible from the moment we'd arrived and piled out of my father's Ford Explorer. I'd been allowed to invite four of my best friends from my neighborhood in Fairfax Village, off Alabama Avenue, and along with my cousins, we had a real party of our own going

1

on. It was a good thing that their home was so large since it seemed like there were a hundred people there.

The sun was still beating down on us even at six P.M. making sure that we all were going to be at least two shades darker. A Keith Sweat tune was blasting through the speakers as the smell of char-broiled meat coasted through the air. Nearly every adult had a cup of liquor or a can of beer in their hands, which only ensured that the party was going to last well into the night.

My friends were having a blast flirting with my male cousins and I didn't blame them. I was always proud of the fact that good looks ran in my family, on both my mother and father's sides. I was happy that Harold, the cousin I was closest to, had invited his new friend from up the street to the cookout. He had to be the most handsome boy I'd ever seen in person. He looked just like Gee Money from *New Jack City.* His name was DeMarcus and I wanted nothing more than for him to be *my* birthday wish. He was sixteen and seemed more mature than my cousins, but being from the city, I was sure that I could keep up with him.

As the girls gathered around while we took a break to eat, I made it known to my friends that DeMarcus was off-limits. When Shante asked, "Nia, how you gonna claim him like that? We all just met him."

My answer was simple. "First off, all the other boys here are my relatives. Second, it's *my* birthday and if you don't like it, you are free to hop your ass on the Metrobus and make the hump back to the city."

She sucked her teeth in disgust and then said, "What about him? You are not related to Jasper."

She was referring to my mother's friend, Julie's son. Jasper had been at every one of my parties and most family functions as long as I could remember and she knew full well

2

that he'd never have a chance with any of us, especially me. "Are you kidding me? Buck toothed Jasper. Do you think for a second I would give his ugly butt some play?" All my girls started laughing. My best friend, Neek, which was short for Dominique, almost choked on her food laughing so hard.

"That ain't right. Ya'll, Jasper is nice." She had been laughing the hardest and was trying to act high minded all of a sudden.

"Nice my ass," I responded. "Nice and retarded."

We finished up our food and talked for twenty minutes before my cousin Harold rolled up on us. "Ya'll wanna play some volleyball? Boys against the girls."

"How about we mix the teams up?" I said. "I want *him* on my team." I was pointing toward DeMarcus.

"It don't matter. You still won't win," Harold shot back. "I'm going to set the net up."

"Alright, we coming."

Ten minutes later I had my back to Demarcus every chance I got to make sure he got a chance to see my behind in my pink and white, polka-dot bikini. I was nicely developed and I was already used to getting way too much attention from the older boys in my neighborhood. Out of my friends, only Neek had a bigger chest, and Shante had slightly more hips and butt, but as far as a total package went, I had the best of both worlds. Plus, Shante's ass was on the verge of being out of shape, while mine was on the verge of being the kind a nigga could set his drink on.

Every time I turned around I caught DeMarcus' eyes scanning my body and it gave me butterflies. At this point I'd kissed a handful of boys and had even been fingered a couple of times, but I hadn't gone all the way yet. Still, the thought of touching DeMarcus excited me. As the game broke up, after we lost I noticed that Shante had been doing everything she could to get his attention, which was starting to irritate me.

When he took a seat by the pool I watched in shock as she took one near him. "Nia," I heard Neek call from behind me. "You better do something. I think Shante's trying to creep."

"She's about to catch an ass whipping out here," I growled.

She shook her head. "Don't fight. It's your birthday."

I looked around at everyone having a good time. I didn't want to ruin the party. Plus I knew my parents would go off if I embarrassed them by getting into it with one of my own friends. I looked at my father who was standing with a group of friends laughing, drinking and arguing about sports as they normally did. From thirty yards away, I heard Mike Tyson's name mentioned, then Evander Holyfield's. As they continued on I scanned the crowd but didn't see my mother. If she didn't see me fighting then I might be able to blame it on Shante.

As I sized her shady tail up I contemplated jumping on her and saying that she swung first but another idea popped into my head. "Neek, I want you to do something for me."

"What?"

"I'm going to go into the house. Once you see me step inside, pull DeMarcus to the side and tell him that I like him *a lot* and that if he wants to get a birthday kiss now would be a good time because I've gone into the house to use the bathroom."

She started giggling. "Are you serious?"

I stood up, gave her a smirk. "You damned right," I said and walked toward the house.

Once I reached the sliding glass door I looked back over at Neek to observe that she had signaled DeMarcus. I ducked

4

inside and looked out the window and my heart began to beat as he looked toward the house before he stood up.

He started toward the house and once again I felt the butterflies in my stomach. I smiled at first out of satisfaction and then caught myself laughing out loud as the expression on Shante's face showed her displeasure at losing his attention. I wondered for a moment if she was going to take off and run after him toward the house. If she did, all bets were off and the beat down would be mandatory.

I ducked around the corner and into the bathroom as I heard DeMarcus opening the door. I timed it so that I'd be coming out of the bathroom as he appeared in front of me. Face to face, he smiled first. I smiled back and he whispered smoothly, "Is this okay?"

I didn't answer as he leaned in and placed his soft lips to mine. This kiss was different than the ones I'd experienced with other boys. There was no goofiness or indecision. He guided me back into the bathroom without ever pulling his lips from mine. The sensations were driving me crazy as his hands were everywhere. I knew instantly that he'd done this more than once. I was now scared at how aggressive he'd become. At the same time, I was getting warm from the feelings his fingertips were sending throughout my body as they brushed along the naked skin on my back.

"You're a good kisser," I was dumb enough to mumble out.

"That's only because I'm kissing you," he said back. Before I knew it he'd moved his mouth to my neck and the new feelings did something new to me and I let out an involuntary moan. "You like that?" he asked.

"Yes," I whispered.

He continued on and before I could react I felt one of his hands slip inside of my bikini and touch my vagina. I gasped and jumped a bit, but he said, "Just relax. It's going to feel good."

His touch excited me and he hadn't been wrong about how good he'd make me feel so I let him continue, and within seconds I'd been penetrated. His finger was sliding in and out of me and I got so wet that I was embarrassed. "Ahhhhh," I moaned uncontrollably.

He continued kissing me. I couldn't believe that I was letting him go so far. With each stroke I drifted farther away from sanity. My parents were outside along with a hundred other people, but I didn't care. This new feeling was the only thing I could focus on.

I didn't even feel him taking my hand until I felt the warm flesh in my palm. Then I looked down to see what had to be at least a six-inch penis. It looked huge to me and I was mesmerized by it. "Go ahead. Rub it," he urged me.

I did. He began to moan. "Nia, that feels good as hell." I watched his eyes in the dimly lit bathroom and I felt strangely powerful. I could tell that I was giving him pleasure. He began to rock forward on his tip toes. "Ahhh," he moaned.

Suddenly he grabbed my hand and guided me back to the counter. I don't know why but I was almost in a state of hypnosis as I allowed him to spread my legs and pull my bikini bottom to the side. The anticipation was so great that I could feel my heartbeat in my throat. I was preparing to tell him to stop when I realized that I couldn't remember his name.

I felt the same hot piece of meat that I'd just finish jerking begin to press at the lips of my pussy. I breathed in deep and felt a twinge of pain as I gave myself away completely for the very first time. An inch at a time he pushed into me. It was the strangest experience of my young life. I was excited, scared and aroused all at once. *DeMarcus*. His name came back to me as he began to stroke in and out of me.

"Oh, Nia. Ohhhhh, ahhhhh," he breathed out. "It feels so good. You have some good pussy," he said between pants for air.

His dirty talk excited me and I got lost in how good he was making me feel. I'd waited for this day for some time. Now, Neek would be the last virgin in my circle of friends. Until it started, I'd never realized how ready to do this I'd been. As I said to myself, *'I'm actually doing this,'* I was jarred back to reality by the sensations that were taking my body over.

Out of nowhere I screamed out, "Fuck me."

"Uhhhhhh," he grunted as his body seemed to lock up. He held on to me as if his life depended on it and then he pulled away and slumped over.

"Are you okay?"

"Yeah," he said softly. He was shaking his head while he tried to regain his composure. "That shit was good."

Shit? I wasn't sure if I liked my sex being referred to in that manner but I decided to take it as a compliment so I smiled. "You go back outside and I'll be out there in a minute."

"Okay. But are you going to give me your phone number?"

"Yeah, I'll get some paper and write it down for you."

He walked back to me and kissed me again. "Happy birthday, Nia."

As he prepared to exit I heard the familiar base of my father's voice outside the door. "Open this door or I'm going to bust it down."

My eyes might as well have hit the floor the way they bugged out. DeMarcus cowered like a puppy and looked as if he was ready to pee on himself. We were both frozen, unsure if we should open the door.

"I know you're in there," he yelled again. My father, Tony, wasn't the biggest man in the world. In fact, he was an inch under six feet tall and no more than two hundred pounds, but I'd never seen anyone in my neighborhood so much as flirt with the idea of disrespecting him, me, or my mother. He had arms that looked like weapons and a face, when frowned up, was as menacing as Darth Vader.

I was shaking my head at DeMarcus apologizing with my facial expression for the beating I feared we were both about to receive. When I heard the boom of a kick I closed my eyes as I crouched. This was followed by the sounds of a door flying open. Next I heard a scream. I recognized this voice as well. It was my mother. This was when I looked up and realized that the bathroom door was still closed.

The screams grew louder and it sounded like furniture was being thrown around. I stood up, motioned DeMarcus out of the way, and pulled the door open. This was when I saw that the door my father had broken down was in the laundry room across the hallway from me.

DeMarcus sliced out from behind me and headed for safety. I rushed into the door behind my father and watched as he was beating Dean, my uncle's business partner, over the head with a beer bottle. My mother was screaming, bloodied in the corner. I didn't understand why she was topless until my father yelled, "You want this bitch? You can have her, but it's gonna cost you."

"Tony, please…" he begged as he held his hands up. I was in shock as my father continued his beating, kicking Dean in the face repeatedly. Dean was lucky that my father had worn sandals instead of the boots he customarily sported all year round. My mother finally tried to stand but my father swung and punched her dead in the nose causing it to erupt into a bloody fountain.

8

"Dadddddeeeeeee, nooooo," I screamed.   My voice halted him and he turned and looked at me. The look in his eyes was like nothing I'd ever seen.

"Nia, go outside," he barked. "You don't need to see this."

"No, please stop. Don't hit her anymore."

My mother was on the floor crying, holding her nose. My father froze for a minute and looked down at her then at Dean, who seemed as if he was having trouble breathing. He reached down and grabbed my mother by her hair and with lighting quickness he reached into a pocket and pulled out a box cutter. Without a second thought, he dragged it across her cheek. She screamed out like a newborn baby and collapsed to the floor.

Then he moved back to Dean and lifted his foot high into the air before bringing it down onto his crotch. With the same blade he took a swipe at Dean's face, but he blocked it with his arm. This seemed to aggravate my father even more as he dragged it down his arm sending a river of blood to pour from his forearm.

Then as if he was suddenly satisfied, he turned to me and said, "I love you, Nia." I stepped back into the door terrified of the butcher who'd appeared in my father's body.

He walked past me with blood all over his shirt and shorts and headed out the door.   I ran to my mother. She was trembling on the ground but wasn't making any noise. I'd learn in the hospital that she'd gone into shock from the pain of having the nerves in her face sliced into.

Dean was moaning and groaning but I paid him no attention as I tried to lift my mother up. While I tried, people began pouring into the house. I heard my Aunt Valerie's voice, "Vernelle, are you okay, baby?" She got no response and Valerie went off, yelling at the top of her lungs. "What did he do to my sister?"

I began to lose my mind, slowly at first. I began to run after my father. I wasn't sure why but when I reached the backyard I saw him coming in my direction. Someone yelled out, "Tony, noooo. Don't do it."

He ran past me back toward the house as people were looking around trying to figure out what was going on. Some of them were still swaying to the sounds of the Isley Brothers' *For the Love of You,* which was playing ironically in the background. "Daddy, what are you doing?" I said as I tried to grab his arm.

It took only a few more seconds for me to realize what he was trying to do once I saw him pull a gun from his pocket. "I'm going to kill that bitch and his punk ass." Everyone screamed as he tried to force his way into the house.

The day went from bad to worse as I heard someone yell, "Drop it, man."

My dad turned around and there was one of the men who he'd been talking to earlier. The man was a Maryland State Trooper and one of Dean's and Wade's friends. He too had a gun and had his pointed directly at my father's face.

My father never looked at me. The last look I remember on his face was one of anger and rage. He fired at the trooper once. The trooper fired four times. Both men fell to the ground as the smell of gunpowder drifted through the air. Once the screaming stopped, everyone in attendance stood around in shock while one person had the sense to call the ambulance and police.

An hour later, the trooper died and my father was lying handcuffed to a bed at Southern Maryland Hospital.

ℒ Right to be Wrong
Chapter 2

Seven months later my mother sat across the table from me in our kitchen delivering words that stung like darts. As she spoke, I wasn't sure which one of us was crazier. *Was she really saying this or was I hallucinating?* My eyes were blinking rapidly, which happened when I got angry. Without realizing it, I'd balled my fist up as I listened to her try to explain to me that not only were we moving, but she was getting married to Dean.

My father had been sentenced only one month earlier and now she had the nerve to tell me that she was moving on, marrying the man she betrayed my father with. As far as I was concerned, both she and Dean had gotten what they deserved. My father, for his part, was convicted of second degree murder, attempted murder and a bunch of other things ranging from possession of, to illegal use of a firearm. In all, that got him a total of life plus thirty years.

My blood started to boil and I felt an instant headache as I thought about the fact that for all practical purposes, I'd lost my father and my virginity on the same day and no one seemed to care. She'd been so busy sneaking around, keeping her ongoing affair a secret that I suppose she never even noticed that it was a struggle everyday for me simply to get out of bed to go to school.

After waking up screaming in the middle of the night, and being rushed to Greater Southeast Hospital, the doctor had referred me for a psych evaluation. I'd gone to a therapist for a few months but our medical coverage only paid for ten sessions. Once the insurance money ran out, my appointments stopped immediately. I'd just begun to get comfortable with the routine of taking sleeping pills to doze off at night and then popping the anti-depressants in the morning so I'd be able to face life. Now, without the meds, I was back to staying up all night and acting like a complete bitch all day, every day.

"Ma, I hate him," I yelled.

"You don't even really know him, Nia. If you just give him a chance you might…"

"Are you fucking crazy?" I yelled as I stood up. My mother now treated me the way white parents did their kids. I was allowed to curse freely whenever I lost my temper. The once stern disciplinarian now accepted my rants as if they were normal. "You want me to give him a chance? Dean disrespected my father. You had sex with him at a cookout on my birthday." I was raving. "Everyone in the neighborhood knows what happened. Do you know how many fights Neek and Brandy have gotten into trying to defend us? People calling you a whore and what not. Now you have the nerve to sit up here and tell me you want to marry that man? You want *me* to give him a chance?" My voice was cracking as the tears began to burn my eyes. "Fuck this."

My mother didn't seem to have an answer. She covered her face and eyes and began to weep like a pained lover. "Nia, I'm so sorry," she cried. "I didn't mean for this to happen."

"Well it did."

"Your father… he and I hadn't been doing well for a long time before that all happened."

"Did he cheat on you? Did he disrespect you and humiliate you the way you did him?"

"I never caught him, but I had reason to believe that he…"

"Don't you do that," I threatened. "Don't sit up here and try to make him out to be a villain when he's not here to defend himself."

My mother's eyes leaked tears. I smirked and got up to leave the kitchen. "Listen Nia. I love Dean and he's going to take us away from here. He's going to move us into a really nice house out in Maryland."

I looked down at her. The scar on her cheek was peering back at me sending chills through me as it reminding me as always why it was there. It was my father's memorial. "You think I care about a house? Ma, my daddy is locked up forever." I stormed into my room and slammed the door behind me. I buried my face in my covers wondering what was going through my mother's brain.

Ten minutes passed when I heard a knock at the door. Thinking it was Neek and Brandy, I poked my head out the door only to be shocked when Dean entered our apartment. He and I locked eyes for the first time since the night of my birthday. I was sure he saw the hatred in my eyes as my lips twisted. I stared for a minute more until I was sure that he saw my father in me, then I turned and walked back into my room.

So you really think you are going to have to move?" Neek asked as we made our way down Southern Avenue seated on the back of the bus.

"I know *she's* going to move. I'm not going anywhere. She can do what the hell she wants. I don't care if I have to live a life of crime. I'll make it on my own." I was staring out the window as we passed the H.O.B.O. clothing shop where a few guys were out front talking. Then an idea popped into my head. "Do you think your mom would let me stay with ya'll?"

"I don't know? I'll ask. We can tell her it's just for the rest of the school year. But then if we get along and don't cause her any trouble, maybe she'll let you stay permanently. It'll be like we're sisters for real."

"We already are," I said as I reached for her hand. "As a matter of fact, we're closer than most sisters I know."

"You know that's for sho'," she said in a cute giggle.

Even after gaining the hope from Neek that I might be able to avoid moving with my mother and Dean, my mind drifted back to the whole idea of her marrying him. Instantly my mood swung like a pendulum and I felt like destroying something.

As the bus traveled toward the subway station I watched as three boys climbed aboard at the next stop. It didn't take a hot minute before they were staring in our direction, all sporting stupid grins. I was used to getting sweated by horny boys every time I turned around, and now that Neek had lost the last of her baby fat and grown nearly three inches in the past five months, she was now commanding the same attention. Her titties were like torpedoes that caused men to eye fuck her every chance they got. She'd always been pretty, now she matched my beauty and I didn't mind the fact that on occasion she might even be able to get more boys than me.

Even with our leather jackets covering our chest, the boys could tell that we were blessed physically, so two of them got up and moved toward us. I wasn't in the mood but I could tell that Neek was totally willing to engage in a conversation with them.

As they slid into seats closest to us the first one asked, "So what's up with ya'll?"

Neek answered, "Nothing, we going to Pentagon City."

"Yeah, us too. Where ya'll from?" the second boy asked.

"Off Alabama Avenue," Neek shot back.

"Gonna do some shopping, huh?" the second one asked.

14

Neek paused and when I didn't chime in she said, "Yeah, a little."

"What's the matter wit' you, shorty? You don't talk?" the first one asked me.

I didn't smile. I just looked at him. He was kind of handsome and I could tell that he was probably used to girls falling all over him. He'd caught me at the wrong time though. I was in a funky mood. I responded, "If I see someone worth talking to, I will."

His man smiled, "Damn, shorty is a trip."

"She just going through some things right now," Neek said on my behalf. The handsome and confident boy in front of me suddenly seemed to morph into a nervous kid searching for the right thing to say to save face in front of his friend.

"My name is Tony. This is Ivan. So what's ya'll name?" When he said his name, I immediately thought of my father.

"Why? You writing a book or are you the police?" I asked.

"I'm Neek and she's Nia," she interjected. I looked at my best friend as if she'd lost her mind, giving out my name to these clowns.

"Nice to meet you. Do ya'll want to catch a movie with us while you guys are out there?"

I shook my head no. Neek responded, "We might not have the time for all that."

Then in a move that I didn't understand, the kid Ivan pulls a wad of cash out of his pocket. "We gonna shop too. If you act halfway nice, we might buy ya'll something."

As if I'd been waiting on a chance to snap, I jumped out there. "Nigga, what makes you think we need your drug money?" I blurted out. "And what makes you think we want to be seen with drug dealers?"

That's when Tony caused me to snap out of my state of nastiness, "Bitch, I'm about tired of your ass already. We trying to be all nice an shit and all you do is keep coming with the bullshit." He stood up and walked back toward the front mumbling, "Fuck them bitches."

I stood up and yelled, "Your mama's a bitch."

He stopped in his tracks and turned around. His buddy seemed to panic. "C'mon, Tony, don't trip. Just chill."

Ivan, confident that Tony wasn't going to come after me, continued talking to Neek. I listened in as he spoke like he had good sense. He complimented her on her beauty but then asked her questions about school and her interest. Neek loved school. From the time we'd walked through the doors, she'd been on a mission to become a cheerleader, join the chorus, the student government, and to basically participate in anything that was school related. Deep down inside she was a nerd, which to me, was one of her best qualities. When Ivan told her that he was in a program called Upward Bound, which was going to help him get into a good college, I knew that Neek was as good as got. Here was a guy who looked like a typical hood, hung out with a guy who called girls *bitches,* yet he was talking about pursuing higher education.

They talked until we got to the subway. He paid for our fare cards and we hopped on the train for the ride into Virginia. I was really impressed when Ivan said, "I'm going to go up here with my boys and let you two talk. Here's my number and my pager, if you need anything let me know." Then he pulled a twenty dollar bill out of his pocket and said. "In case I don't see you at the mall, I want to treat you both to lunch."

Ivan was a real gentleman. Even in my mood there was nothing bad I could say about him. As he joined his friends in the front of the train, Tony and I exchanged glances and I imagined what he was thinking as he shot me a cold, blank,

16

stare. He wasn't the first, and I figured he surely wouldn't be the last man that wouldn't like my style.

Just to let him know that I wasn't intimidated, I mouthed the words, *'Fuck you.'* I wasn't backing down. He stared back at me for another five seconds and then he smiled before turning away as if he'd paid me no mind.

On My Own
Chapter 3

By the time spring reached full effect my mother was so busy trying to have a life that she'd all but forgotten about me. Now that her divorce from my father was final, all she could think about was her wedding. Things had gotten bad between us so I didn't meet much resistance when I packed up and left my mother's house for days at a time as she prepared for her big day with Dean.

Neek's mom, Miss Patty, I called her, had all but let me move in with them, but that arrangement came to an end abruptly when Neek got caught skipping school having sex with Ivan. Her mother came home from work early and caught her bent over in the shower with Ivan plowing into her. She didn't come right out and say it but I knew she blamed me for Neek's change in behavior. She should have blamed the dick. Neek was sprung and that didn't have anything to do with me. Miss Patty had to know that good dick will make a little girl start doing all kinds of grown up stuff. Get her thinking she's a *woman* when she's still a kid.

Lucky for me, I guess, my mother hadn't given up our apartment yet. It seemed more luck for her best friend, Julie, and her son, the buck-toothed retard, Jasper. They were the victims of a fire three weeks before my mom was to marry Dean.

She let Julie move into our two bedroom on the condition that I be allowed to keep my room and stay there until the end of the school year. It took a little getting used to, having Jasper in the house. But to be honest, I liked the arrangement. Julie stayed out of my way and Jasper was so quiet that if I wasn't tripping over him every time I walked past the sofa, where he slept and kept himself planted every waking moment, I wouldn't have known he was there.

During the next few months it seemed as if I'd slowly began to raise myself, barely talking to my mother and never giving Julie the level of respect that I probably should have. Though she was the closest thing I had to a legal guardian once my mother married Dean. I never asked permission, I simply *told* her what I was doing.

It was the week of spring break and as usual, I announced to Julie that I was heading out to Neek's for the night. She'd been on punishment forever and a day it seemed since she'd gotten caught fucking. I met her on the corner at the halfway point between our apartments. Together we trotted the two blocks to where Ivan and Tony were waiting. Tony smiled as I approached the car.

"Hey, sexy," he said.

"Hey you," I smiled back as I approached the door. Neek piled in the back and we pulled off slowly as he leaned in for a kiss. I quickly Frenched him, tongues swirling deep inside of each other's mouths and then we pulled away as if one of us had a plane to catch. I'd never expected Tony and I to end up together after the way we met, but they say persistence breaks down resistance and so it was with he and I. Ivan and Neek had been inseparable since they'd met. Ivan and Tony were always together, so even though we didn't like each other at the start, we found ourselves constantly in each other's company. With all the tagging along as the third and fourth wheel, he and I wound up kicking it by default.

Tony wasn't as bad as I thought initially. Not only was he handsome, the boy could actually hold a decent conversation as long as I kept the subject off of anything that had to do with school. Best of all, he kept a pocket full of money. Even though I didn't really care for the tough guy routine he was always trying to portray, I got used to it. He was a die-hard 2Pac fan and was doing his best to live the thug life.

"Ya'll hungry?" Ivan asked as we headed out towards Virginia.

"Always," Neek replied.

"Good, we gonna hit a seafood spot out in Alexandria before we hit the hotel then," Tony said.

They were always taking us to nice restaurants. It was like we were dating grown men. Ivan, with his intellectual side, always had some fascinating intellectual conversation. Tony, for his part, carried himself like a man who'd done ten years in jail and was now living life as if there was no tomorrow.

I couldn't believe that Neek was now so willing to give her goodies up on demand, but it was clear that Ivan had her nose wide open. She'd gone from the last virgin on the block to his fuck toy.

I wasn't sure if it was the trials I'd faced in the last nine months, or hanging around Tony all the time, but I'd changed too. I knew that I'd started to get wild. For starters, I was drinking every time we hung out and once I'd let Tony become my second lover, I couldn't front, I wanted sex all the time. At first I think it was simply the rush I felt during the act that helped me escape the pain in my life, but as time went on, I'd started to realize that I simply loved the way a hot penis felt inside of me.

At the Chart House, an upscale seafood restaurant, near the water front, we ate steak and lobster tails. I watched in amazement as Tony pulled out a huge wad of cash to pay the three hundred dollar tab before we jetted out of the restaurant. A short while later we pulled into the parking lot of the Holiday Inn on Telegraph Road.

We sat in the car while Ivan went in and secured the rooms. He came back out and Neek's eyes lit up as if she'd hit the lottery. She was in love. "It's about damn time," Tony said. "Where's my change?"

Ivan handed him a twenty and a key. "Pull around to the back," he said. "The rooms are on the other side."

Once we parked the two of them climbed out of the car, stepped a few feet away from us, and began to talk amongst themselves. Tony burst into laughter as Ivan shook his head 'no'. I paid them no attention.

A few moments later I watched as Neek and Ivan entered their room, five doors up the hall. Tony and I entered our door and the first thing I noticed was that the room was ice cold. "Who the hell left the air-conditioner on like it's summer out there?"

Tony laughed. "Don't worry, I'ma heat you up." Then he went over and cut it off, turning on the heat. "I'ma take a shower real quick, you wanna get in with me?"

I nodded as I continued rubbing my shoulders trying to keep warm. He switched the clock radio on to WPGC, and turned the lights off. Silk's *Loose Control* was playing. I loved that song and started to feel sexy as soon as the words started flowing from the tiny box. It was almost ten P.M. and the only light in the room was shining in through the curtains from outside.

Even still I could see clearly as Tony began to strip. He pulled off his shirt and then I watched as his jeans and boxers dropped to the floor together. "Take your clothes off." He smiled at me and headed into the bathroom.

I wasn't shy. The fact of the matter was that Tony's attention only caused me to gain even more confidence in my body. When I walked into the bathroom and stood in front of the mirror I could see Tony's reflection, even with the steam now covering the glass. He was staring at me from the shower. I slid my skin-tight, yellow, Guess jeans off and watched how hungry Tony looked as my thick bottom began to pop out of the top of my jeans. I took my time, wiggling my ass a bit, as I fought to get the jeans down to my ankles.

I pretended to be looking at my lips in the mirror as I pulled my shirt off and unhooked my bra. Still moving slowly, I turned slightly to the side giving him a side view of my beautiful, 34D globes. "Hey, come on. Hurry up," he said. I'd had my fun torturing him. I dropped my panties and turned to face him.

Once I climbed into the hot water I reached for him to steady myself as my feet hit the bottom of the tub. As I turned to soak my body, I brushed up against him and discovered that he was already rock hard. The beads of steaming water pelted my shoulders and sent the chill rushing from my body. Still, my nipples stood off my chest as if I were at the North Pole. Tony grabbed me by the waist and pulled me to him. He landed a kiss on me and he began groping my body as if he hadn't touched a woman in months.

"Let me wash up first, Tony," I begged.

He backed away and smiled. "Let me help." He grabbed the bar of soap, made a handful of lather and went predictably for my breast. He spun me around and soaped me up while I pushed my rear end into his crotch.

"Is this what you want?" I asked seductively.

"Hell yeah," he whispered.

It didn't take long for me to get turned on, especially when Tony acted so aggressively. "Then get it," I said.

22

I didn't have to tell him twice as he grabbed me by my hair and forced me to bend over. I held onto the sides of the tub as I felt the tip of his dick pushing into my pussy. He wasn't graceful, instead I felt as if he was in a race to fuck my brains out. A few slow and ordered strokes to start with was all I got before he began smashing in and out of me. I wasn't as turned on as he was to start, but I began to catch up as he began to groan and talk with the nasty lingo I'd begun to love. "Nia, this pussy is so good."

All I did was grunt and return with, "Fuck me. Fuck me."

"Oh yeah. Take my dick, Nia. Take it."

"Fuck me harder, Tony. Fuck this pussy."

"It's soooo tight."

Through the furious action, I had to fight to keep my balance in the shower. Nearly slipping didn't stop me from urging him to hit it harder.

He continued to bang for a few moments more before he grunted out, "Ahhhhhhhhhh yeaahhhhhh." He slammed into me a few times before pulling his limp penis from inside of me. Leaning under the water he said, "That shit was good."

I nodded, more winded than satisfied. I hoped he have another few rounds in him.

I stepped out of the shower, took a seat on the toilet and forced myself to pee and do my best to squeeze my vaginal muscles to force his cum out of me. Tony had taught me this method of birth control. He called this 'making the booty spit up'. I climbed back into the shower as he was getting out. It took me another five minutes to wash up and get fresh for him again. After I finished, I headed to the bed to join him and found him flat on his face already snoring. I took it as a compliment and slid onto the bed next to him.

I didn't bother looking at the clock. Instead I closed my eyes as I listened as Brownstone played on the radio. I assumed that as usual, Tony would wake me for another round or two, or at least I hoped since I had some energy left to burn. With that thought I drifted off beside him.

We couldn't have been asleep for more than thirty minutes when a series of hard knocks came at the door. I was startled as Tony sat up in the bed. "What the fuck?" he mumbled out.

He got up and walked to the door to look out the peep hole. "Who is it? Is it Ivan?" I asked.

"No it ain't," he said as he backed away from the door. "Shit, shit, shit," he repeated in a whisper.

"What's wrong?" I asked as the knocks came again.

"It's a guy I know named Ali. I owe him some money."

"Well how did he know you were here?"

"I'm not sure. Maybe somebody saw me walking in," he shot back. "He has a lot of eyes in this town."

"Well don't let him come…"

I was interrupted by another set of knocks. "Tee, I know you in there."

I watched as Tony quickly put his clothes on and said, "I'ma step outside. You just chill, I'll be back in minute after I talk with him."

Tony opened the door. "Hey, Ali," I heard him say and like a scene out of a movie I watched him start backing into the room with his hands up in front of his face. Ali held a pistol aimed at him and when he looked over at me he shook his head giving me the feeling that I was in the wrong place at the wrong time. I began to panic as I thought about the night my father was shot.

"I'm not here to do a bunch of talking," Ali barked. "Do you have my money?"

"I have most of it, but not on me. I have everything but two G's."

"That's not good, homes," he said. "I'll tell you what. I'll sit here with your girl and if you come back with all of it in an hour or less, then everything is cool. If you don't, then shit is gonna get super ugly." His tone was deathly serious. He looked to be at least twenty years old with a mustache and goatee. Tony looked to have gotten himself into trouble with a grown man. Ali stood around six feet tall and had the body of an athlete. Tony wasn't a slouch but it looked as though Ali could have easily taken him without a gun.

I was too scared to speak. Instead I thought about my clothes on the bathroom floor. I was covered in a sheet but I felt more naked than I'd ever been. I couldn't believe what I heard next when Tony said, "Just don't hurt her. I'll get the money."

My eyes nearly bugged out of my head as I stared at him. *Are you really going to leave me alone with this man?* I was still yet to say a word. The fear had literally paralyzed my vocal chords. "Nia, I'll be right back. I promise."

Ali took a seat as if he'd paid for the room and set his gun on the table. He looked at his watch and said, "One hour. You got one hour."

Tony stood staring at me for a second. My eyes watered as I wished I'd never gotten involved with him. It was at that moment that I realized that I didn't really even like him all that much, at least not enough to be held hostage for his drug debt.

"Time is fucking ticking," Ali said. Then he added, "Tony, you know how I roll. If you don't come back, I might start with her, but I won't stop there. As easy as I found you here, I know where your sister lives, your grandmother's house…"

"Man, I told you I got you," he said. With a pitiful look on his face he added, "Nia, I'm sorry, I'll be right back." He picked his keys up and headed for the door.

Still in the bed, I laid there for a couple of minutes as Ali and I made eye contact. He pulled out a joint and lit it. "Maria," he said as he took the first puff. "I'm not going to hurt you. I just want him to think I will so that he'll bring my money. I would hurt him though," he added.

He took a couple more pulls of the weed. I looked into his eyes. I believed his words. I don't know why but I corrected him. "Nia. My name is Nia, not Maria."

He nodded, "Yeah, whatever." He looked at his watch again. "You smoke?"

I shook my head, "No."

"Well try it. It'll help you relax." I didn't respond so he added, "It's harmless. Really it is. Just try a little puff."

"No thanks, really."

His face frowned up a bit and then he insisted, "Come on. You can trust me." I didn't want to, but I was nervous as hell and I didn't want to offend or anger him. He moved over to the bed and extended his arm toward me with only his fingertips holding the joint. "Why the fuck your hands shaking like that? You got a nervous condition or something?" he asked as I reached for it.

I shrugged my shoulders and took the joint from him. "I guess I'm a little nervous."

"Fuck that. I told you I'm not going to do nothing to hurt you as long as you stay cool." I put it to my mouth and he said, "Pull the smoke into your mouth then inhale real slow like."

I sucked the smoke down my throat. It burned and I began to cough uncontrollably. He laughed at me as my eyes began to water. "Try it again," Ali said.

The second time I pulled softer and the cannabis slid into my lungs much more smoothly. Instantly I felt different. I actually felt good, instantly mellow; no longer scared or

26

nervous. Ali had given me something good I believed. I looked at him and for the first moment since he'd been in the room I realized that he wasn't scary, but rather handsome and strong. I smiled, closed my eyes, and embraced that I liked the way I felt. Discovering that drugs can help you get through an uncomfortable situation was like riding a raft over a waterfall. Life would never be the same after that.

Twenty minutes later I was wondering what in God's name he'd given me to smoke. My head was spinning as if I were on a ride at Six Flags. I never imagined that marijuana would get my head going like it was now. I was two steps beyond relaxed. I felt like I was sailing in the clouds and I really had nothing to go on except for my guesses as to what it would feel like being high.

What confirmed for me that I wasn't in my right mind was when Ali leaned in and kissed me. I didn't resist him. Instead I pulled away after a couple of seconds and started laughing. "What are you doing?" I asked still giggling.

"What do you think?" he answered back. "You're sexy."

"Yeah, thanks, but I'm too young for you."

"Well what are you doing in this hotel room naked, if you're *too* young?" I sat silent

He had a good point. I stood up to go to the bathroom to retrieve my clothes forgetting that I was buck naked. "You're right. I need to go. I gotta get my clothes."

When he saw my body he yelled out, "Oh shit, girl. You stacked like a motherfucker." I might have blushed at the compliment, but before I could he jumped up in front of me blocking my path. "You ain't goin no fucking where."

"Please let me go." He slid to the side out of my path and I tried to make it past him when he reached for my pony tail and yanked me back to the bed. Instantly my heart began to beat. "Get off of me," I huffed out.

He grabbed me and pulled my mouth to his. He forced my lips apart and began to tongue me into submission. His hands were all over my body and my first instinct was to pull away but when he reached for my pussy, he found a puddle on my outer lips. He sent two fingers inside of me and almost lifted me off the ground by my vagina.

The fear was about to set in as he shoved me onto my back. The drugs had me moving as if I was in quicksand. He pulled his shirt over his head and dropped his pants to the ground in a matter of seconds. I watched in the now dimly lit room as his meat escaped from his boxers. He had a pole hanging between his legs and I had to adjust my eyes to make sure I wasn't seeing things.

"Ali, please let me get my clothes," I pleaded in my most sincere voice. If he'd have let me, I would have rushed to put them on. He didn't and instead he climbed onto the bed and pinned me down. He started with the kissing again and this time I began to tremble, a mix of fear, shame and excitement rushing through me at once. I would wait for the right moment and try to break free.

He fondled my breasts, licking my Hershey-brown nipples until they were like missiles ready to launch. Then he began to finger me again while I tried to resist the urge to moan out in pleasure. When I couldn't I jerked away and kicked him. I rolled off of the bed on the other side and prepared to make a run for the bathroom. "I'm going to yell rape," I threatened.

"And I will kill you."

It was then that I realized his gun was on the table. I looked over at it and as my feet began to move toward it, he lunged out at me and grabbed my shoulders and hair once

28

again. This time he hurt me as he used a firm grip. "Now you done pissed me off you little bitch," he whispered. "I was going to go easy on you, but now..."

He didn't finish his sentence. His strength became apparent as he locked his hand on my jugular and began to choke the shit out of me. A minute later he had me flat on my back, hand still on my throat as he separated my thighs. My chest was heaving as the tears began to come. He wasn't tuned in to my feelings as he rubbed the head of his huge dick at the opening of my treasure. He tried to push it in and I flinched. It wasn't going to fit.

The next thing I felt was his goatee brushing against my thighs. It tickled slightly, but the feeling of his hair on my skin was nothing compared to the moment his tongue brushed against my clit. I had never experienced such sensations like this. Three licks and my clit was swollen, even though I tried to fight it. Once he realized my body was responding, his assault on my pearl became even more deadly. Though my hands were free, I didn't use them to fight or try to push him away.

Again, I held back the signs of pleasure as best I could, but he ate me like he was being paid for it. I began to breathe like a marathon runner struggling toward the finish line. Then I began to gasp as if all the air were being sucked out of the hotel room. His hands slid from my ankles to my ass and I thought about trying to buck away, but the heat of his tongue and his ability to use it the way Michelangelo used a paint brush, unleashed the tiny bolts of electricity that would surely clear the path for a body stirring orgasm. I'd already learned how to give myself one that was intense, but I'd yet to have one delivered to the magnitude that I felt approaching.

I opened my eyes and looked down at the top of his head. He was so into sucking me inside out, that I forgot that I was in the middle of being raped. I became nothing but a lump of flesh wanting to hump his face. "Oh shit," I yelled as a spark hit me.

"Mmmmhmmmm," he mumbled nose deep in my hole.

"Nooooo… please," I cried out. The juices were pouring out of me; mine mixed with his saliva, out of my girl, between my ass cheeks and onto the bed so rapidly that it didn't even make sense.

With no attempt at finesse, he suddenly jammed four fingers inside of me, stretching my hole into a new state of arousal. "Fuck," I yelled out.

"I'm getting you ready for this monster," he barked out. More licking and finger fucking followed until he caused me to start to spasm. My eyes rolled up into my head and I lost myself to the orgasm. It started in my chest and ripped down through my stomach muscles. I wanted to grab his head and pull his tongue deeper into my pussy but I was paralyzed. I felt so controlled, so helpless.

I thought about his aggression, how he'd begun to devour me as if I were no more than a piece of meat. With my mind stuck on how he'd taken control of my body and like a river raging over rocks, I came so incredibly hard.

"Ahhhhhh, shiiit," I panted out over and over as my ass took on a mind of its on and started bouncing off of the bed to meet the thrust of his tongue.

I didn't know if it was Ali, the weed or a combination, but the cumming had me seeing colors inside of my eyelids as my pussy officially turned into a water ride. Orange, white, yellow, red.

"Ouch," he said. I hadn't realized how violently I had shaken until he screamed out. My eyes opened and I gazed into his. During my ass-bucking orgasm, he'd bitten his tongue.

Still, he smiled as he moved up the bed toward me. I was still reeling from my orgasm but I knew that he was about to fuck me. I momentarily came back into my senses and made it off the bed once again. My knees were wobbly still from the pleasure that had wracked my body. So I moved like a wounded animal as I tried to make it past him. Once again, I felt his hands pulling my hair. He led me back but stopped short of throwing me down onto the bed. With his forearm he folded me over onto my knees and he positioned himself behind me. My knees were locked together as I tried to cross my legs under me, but it did no good. I was slightly bow-legged and had a heart shaped ass. When I bent over like this, my pussy was open like a garage door.

Ali couldn't have known this detail of my anatomy but still he took advantage of the easy access pressing the thick head of his dick to my opening and plunging in.

I imagined my Tony walking into the room seeing me bent over like this. I wondered what he'd think about my moaning out in pleasure as Ali fucked me and groped my breasts.

'Only a whore would enjoy this', I thought to myself. I felt pounds of guilt with each delicious stroke. It wasn't my fault. I hadn't cheated, but I couldn't deny. I loved it and I was both surprised and disgusted with myself at the same time.

I never imagined that I would enjoy being fucked like this. My knees were bent slightly as Ali slammed into me rhythmically. I wanted more, deeper and harder.

"Fuck me…" I grunted wishing I could massage my own nipples, but he'd pulled my hands behind my back.

"What?" he shot back. His hand firmly wrapped up in my hair. If I'd had a weave it would have given way with his yanking. "What did you say?" he panted.

"Ohhhhh," I moaned.

31

"Say it again. Come on, bitch."

I had never had anyone talk to me like that. I winced as his vulgarity took me higher. He proceeded to bang me for ten minutes straight. His pistoning in and out sent me to the edge a couple of times but I felt something bubbling inside of me on its' way out.

"Ohhh, gawwd," I was fighting for air as the pillows underneath me pressed up against my abdomen. He leaned in more and smashed my face into the mattress. "Fuck me. K…k…k…keeeep fuggin' me."

"Yeah, bitch you love it. Tell me you love it."

"Ahhhhh, ahhhhh…" another orgasm was approaching.

"Say it," he yelled as he slammed it in balls deep.

"I love it," I yelled over and over as I came all over his dick.

I felt my self ready to black out but fought to stay with him and give him the release I now felt he deserved. I clenched my young muscles. With the third squeeze he moaned out, "I'm coming, shorty." The pace of his pumps quickened to turbo and he exploded, all up inside my womb.

I loved what he'd done to me and the feel of his spasms sent me over the top once more. I pushed my backside into him causing my cheeks to clap when we collided. He was now the helpless one as he humped through another orgasm until he nearly collapsed. We melted into each other and dozed so spent that my lying in the wet spot didn't even matter.

When I woke up two hours later I hadn't heard the door open, but I heard as it slammed shut. A second later Tony was standing at the foot of the bed. I looked up at him and then over at Ali who was still sleeping beside me, ass naked.

"Oh shit," I said realizing Tony could see that I'd allowed Ali to fuck me silly a while earlier.

Tony's eyes locked with mine as he came to the realization of what had happened. In a voice that showed his complete shock at the scene before him he simply yelled out, "What the fuck?"

Road Rage
Chapter 4

On the morning of my sixteenth birthday Ali drove me out to Washington Boulevard in Arlington, Virginia. He promised me that he had a surprise for me that I'd never forget. After admiring a tennis bracelet I'd seen at a jewelry store a couple of weeks prior, I thought we were headed to Ballston Commons to pick it up, but I was wrong. I'd forgotten the scenery on the way to the mall for the fact that it never meant much to me as a fifteen year old.

When we pulled into the car lot on Clarendon Boulevard, my eyes widened. We hopped out of Ali's Pathfinder, a foreigner practically tripped over his own feet trying to get out of the tiny office onto the lot. He smiled and said, "Ali, my man, you're early."

"Huh?"

"The car's almost ready. I told you I was going to have it detailed for you. It'll be looking like new. It will be here by noon. How about I buy you lunch and…"

"We'll be back in an hour," Ali said. He handed him a lump of cash, "That's the rest."

"Thank you, Ali."

We pulled off and drove toward the mall. Ali looked pissed. "What's wrong, baby?" he loved when I called him baby.

"These damn Saddam Hussein looking motherfuckers. I told them I wanted the car ready when we pulled up. I wanted to surprise you."

"With a car?" he nodded. "Oh my gawd, Ali. A car," I screamed all giddy. "What kind?"

"At least that will be a surprise. You'll see when we get back."

I'd gotten to know a lot about Ali over the past couple of months. He was strong and commanded respect in the streets. He was also extremely loyal and kind to the few people he dealt with. It took him a little while to open up, but when he did tell me a little about his family life, I felt bad for him. After moving from Pittsburgh to D.C. as a toddler, his mother ran into a string of bad luck. She turned to drugs, got into an abusive relationship and forgot all about him, until he started getting into trouble. By the time Ali turned eleven he'd had a rap sheet several pages long. Tired of Social Services on her back, his mother moved without telling him when he was fourteen.

Ali wound up living with his uncle until he was fifteen. He'd been on his own since then. From that point on, he bounced from couch to couch until he got into a relationship with his case worker. She'd taken him in after seeing the size of his penis during a urine test. She was fifteen years older than him and still she cried like a baby the day he left her to marry the streets.

Ali never said it, but I figured that at the very least, she'd schooled him in the art of making love. He loved sex and could fuck like a champion. In fact, I felt like he'd taught me more than any girl my age should know about sex, but most of all he was generous. Even still, I couldn't believe he was buying me a car after only knowing me for such a short while.

As we pulled into the garage I thought about that night when Tony came back to the hotel with Ali's money. Ali took the hundred dollars that Tony had paid for the room out of the stack and handed it to him. Then as if he had every right to do so, he told Tony to 'bounce'.

Tony had stared at me like a puppy dog and said, "Come on, Nia. Get dressed."

"Nah, without her. She wit' Ali now," he'd responded.

I said nothing. A part of me was scared of how it would all turn out, but I couldn't fake. My pussy wanted to stay with Ali. So I didn't move.

Tony's voice was cracking as he said, "Ali, I paid you, man. That's my girl."

Ali just laughed. "Man, she ain't your girl. Plus you don't want to hit that after me. She just took ten and a half, *thick* inches, with no problem," he gloated.

Tony looked at me as if I were scum. I sat up in the bed and stared back at him as I witnessed a familiar look. His pride had been destroyed and he wore the same expression that my father had after catching my mother and Dean. Only Tony didn't have the heart that my father did. Instead of regaining his dignity through animalistic means, he turned and walked away.

The next morning, Ali taught me how to properly give a blow job. I tried to pull away when he came but he held my head on his shaft as he filled my mouth with his seed. After that, he'd insisted on me choking down his meat as a precursor to sex nearly every time.

Through the period where Ali called himself 'breaking me in', the rough sex continued and I loved every minute of it.

We spent an hour in the mall but didn't find anything worth buying other than a few CD's. My mind was on the car. I couldn't wait to see what he'd bought for me. When we pulled back up at the lot there was a champagne-colored, Acura Legend coupe. It really did look brand new. I was so excited that I jumped up and down and screamed. "Thank you, baby. Thank you so, much."

Ali let out the rare smile and said, "You're welcome. Now all you have to do is get your license. I'm going to take you this afternoon."

I was in heaven as I followed Ali down Glebe Road headed back toward I-395. I popped in the TLC's *Crazy Sexy Cool* CD and skipped to my favorite song, *Waterfalls*. I was blasting the music as I cruised behind his truck as if I'd been driving for years. It was my day and I couldn't wait to get back around the way to show my girls my new whip.

When we made it to my street, Ali parked his truck and climbed in with me. He looked over at me with a stern look. I paid close attention to his expression. With his dark skin, he reminded me of the younger Michael Jordan, the tongue wagging one with hair. I thought he was a beautiful specimen, even though he was a little scary at times, always seeming like he was holding back some deep, dark, side of his personality.

"Okay these are the rules."

I sat there waiting, ready for him to tell me what time to be in the house every night and how many times a day I'd have to check in. "Uh huh," I said willing to obey anything he asked.

He paused and smiled again, "Just have fun and enjoy the car." Then he added, "But be careful."

I smiled and leaned in and kissed him. "So are we gonna practice my parking now?"

"In just a minute. Right now, I want you to pull around the corner and pull the car through the alley." Driving slowly, I obliged him until he told me where to stop. He climbed out and motioned for me to join him behind the car.

Once I stood before him he grabbed a fistful of my hair, his trademark move. In one swift motion, he turned me around, bending me over the trunk of the car. With his free hand he pulled my jean skirt up and yanked my panties clean off.

"Stop. Someone will see us," I clamored.

"Shut the fuck up," he snapped back. A second later, my eyes were rolling up into my head as he pushed his dick inside of me right there in broad daylight.

As usual, he set me off on a journey to orgasmic delight. He pounded me without shame as my pussy began to throb. A minute into his fucking me someone walked up the alley. It was a couple, a woman and a man with a shopping bag in his hand. I was completely embarrassed. "They're going to see us," I said in a whisper."

It didn't bother Ali as he continued on. I wanted to turn invisible once they made it to us. The woman stopped stunned at the sight of our lovemaking. She grabbed her man by the arm. I didn't recognize either of them, thank goodness. I heard him say, "Damn."

She followed with, "James, come on. Fucking nasty ass hoe."

Her words didn't shame me. The fact they were watching actually turned me on in some strange way. My pussy began to do somersaults and I relaxed enough to have a small orgasm as Ali emptied himself all over my ass cheeks. Sweating like a pig, I jumped off of the hot car and climbed into the passenger seat as fast as possible.

I didn't say a word as we drove off. After five minutes of silence he looked over at me and turned the music down. "What you mad?" he asked.

Not saying a word, I turned and looked out the window, smiling. Every now and then I liked playing the mad role. It usually got him trying hard to spoil me in an effort to make up to me. A few seconds before I let him know that I wasn't mad he said, "Hey, after you pass the test, let's go get that bracelet you wanted."

On top of that, he was beyond patient as we practiced my driving and parallel parking in the RFK Stadium parking lot.

An hour later with his dried cum all over my ass, I passed my driver's test. Our next stop was the mall.

Shante was way too pressed to read my registration. When she saw *Nia Morgan* on the temporary registration her face got tighter than a weightlifter's ass. "What, bitch, you thought I was lying?" I laughed as I reached back into the back seat to retrieve the slip from her.

Neek was of course, riding shotgun, and Brandy was in the back with Shante. We were painting the town red in celebration of my birthday. I had a pocket full of money, compliments of Ali, and was looking like a million dollars rocking a pair of Dolce & Gabbana jeans, a BCBG shirt and a fresh pair of Gucci sneakers. Without thinking twice, I'd introduced my crew to the potent weed that Ali gave me. He bragged that he had some peeps from Humboldt County in California. It was a place I couldn't have pointed out on a map, but I did know they had some of the strongest weed in the country. At least Ali preached that every time he inhaled the cheeba, and I believed him.

Me and my girls didn't smoke enough to lose our minds right away, but we did get high enough to get the munchies. We saved the rest of the smoke for the ride to the club just in case we couldn't get a drink once we got inside the club.

I was pissed when we couldn't get into Houston's with out an adult but we wound up at TGI Friday's on Pennsylvania Avenue, near George Washington University. Acting like we hadn't eaten in weeks, we ordered a bunch of food that we practically inhaled before going to a club out in Maryland called The Classics. The Northeast Groovers were playing and the place was bound to be packed.

The line was out the door as we cruised into the lot. I felt like a celebrity about to walk the red carpet as the bystanders were all staring at us as we pulled up. Sometimes everything went right, and this was one of those times. There was a parking space right on the font row near the door waiting for me. I backed in carefully and we sat there for a moment making sure our hair was in place and that our lip gloss was perfect.

"Ya'll bitches ready?" I asked.

"You know it," Brandy shot back.

We climbed out and we were greeted with a chorus of 'Damns' and 'Hey, Shortaaaay's' from the niggas in line. I couldn't blame them or the older chicks who I overheard using words like teenie boppers. Hell, we were that, but boppers or not, my jeans were fitting so damn perfect that I could have stopped traffic, caused a wreck and gotten a ticket. Neek's titties were on display as usual in her low-cut sun dress and Brandy, though slim as she was, was stunningly pretty. She had a face like Pocahontas. Shante, who I thought usually dressed like a skank, even looked good in her yellow Versace jeans and the halter top that she was rocking.

We walked straight to the door and I told the doorman that Ali had sent us and he let us in, no charge, no id. Once we made it in I found a table near the windows in the front of the club. The room was shaped like a space ship with windows covering every wall. I greeted Ali's connect at the club, a guy named J.R. once he noticed us. A few minutes later J.R. had a waitress bring a cake and a bottle of Moet from the kitchen.

I couldn't believe it when he told me that Ali had the cake delivered. In pink icing the cake read, happy 21st birthday on it. Ali knew good and well that I was sweet sixteen, but that wouldn't have flown to well at the club. We had a blast sipping the bubbly, clicking glasses and acting like grown ass women.

The party was just getting started when I heard a familiar voice from behind me. "Happy birthday, cousin."

I looked up and it was my cousin Harold, two of his friends that I didn't recognize, and none other than DeMarcus. I jumped up and hugged him, "Heeeyyyyy, Harooollllld," I said.

"Girl, you pissy drunk, ain't you?"

"*Ain't* ain't a word, my nigga," I giggled.

"So what's up? I see you doing it big, sipping on the Mo and what not."

"That ain't nothing. Check these out," I said as I dangled my keys up. I caught DeMarcus staring at me, but I ignored him.

"What you got there?"

"Come here." I grabbed his hand and pulled him to the window. "You see that right there? That's my new ride."

"Yeah, right," he said.

"Do I got to take you out there to see the registration? That's my shit. My nigga bought it for me."

"It's like that?"

"It's like *that*," I shot back.

"Well, it looks like life is treating you swell."

"I can't complain. Come on, have some cake, it's good as shit."

We rejoined the crowd and as I should have expected Shante was all up in DeMarcus' face. I don't know if it was the liquor, or me feeling territorial, but I rolled up on him and squeezed his ass.

He jumped as if he had been violated and turned around. I started laughing. Shante rolled her eyes and I laughed at her letting her know that I didn't give a damn how she felt. "Hey, Nia," DeMarcus said.

"Long time, no hear from," I said.

"Yeah, it's been a while. Happy birthday, by the way."

"Thanks."

He and I had tried to keep in contact after the cookout but with everything I had been going through with my father I was to emotionally spent to allow him to bond with me the way he was trying. Eventually, I wore him out. A little more than a month after we'd met and I'd given him my virginity, the phone calls and interest seemed to trail completely off.

"So you been alright, I hear?" DeMarcus asked.

"You hear?"

"Yeah, Shante just told me your man copped you a brand new Acura coupe for your birthday."

I smacked my lips and looked at her real hard. She turned away. "Something like that. So what's up? You want to get on the floor with the birthday girl?"

"We can definitely do that."

I took DeMarcus by the hand and waved for everyone else to follow us to the floor. "It's on now ya'll," Brandy yelled out.

A minute later, after trudging through the crowd we all made our way on to the floor and began to dance. It seemed more like we were swaying together like a church choir since we were all jammed together like sardines and there was no room to really dance.

Staring into DeMarcus' face I was taken back to when I'd first laid eyes on him. Even though both of our lives had kept moving, I hadn't forgotten him. He put his hands on my waist and his eyes looked as if he'd drifted off somewhere far away. "Are you okay?" I leaned in close to his ear and asked him.

"Yeah, why do you ask?"

"You look like something is on your mind," I said back.

"It's just that you look so good. I mean you've grown like shit. I can't believe it. You was tight last year, but now you have a body like one of those chicks from the videos."

"I guess that's a compliment."

He smiled and said, "You've gotten even prettier and your body has..." He didn't finish his sentence before I felt something wet splash across my face. I broke the embrace and noticed that DeMarcus had a liquid running down the side of his face as well. We looked over and there was none other than Tony standing there with an empty glass in his hand laughing.

I looked around to see if Ivan was nearby and how he'd managed to let his monkey get out of control, but I didn't see him. Instead I saw a bunch of other thuggish-looking guys surrounding Tony, they'd probably given him some courage, but still I wasn't scared. I'd seen the real Tony that night in the hotel.

"Nigga what the fuck is your problem?" I asked.

"My bad, ya'll," he laughed and then added, "It slipped."

"You's a punk ass nigga," I barked.

"I said it slipped, bitch. Don't get slapped up in here."

DeMarcus stepped in front of me and said, "Man, you ain't gonna slap nobody over here."

"Slim, I know you ain't trying to fight for this freak bitch. She's a whore."

"Man, fuck you, you don't know her."

"Oh, I know her freak ass. My man know her, and my other man too. We ran a G on her ass," he said lying. "Everybody round the way know Miss Nia."

DeMarcus looked at me with disappointment on his face as if he was contemplating believing Tony's story. "That nigga is lying." I turned to Tony and said, "I'ma tell Ali and he is going to fuck you up. He is going to light your bitch ass up and make you cry again. Yeah, nigga, I heard you cried like a bitch."

With that comment his face frowned up and he lunged for me, only to be wobbled by DeMarcus' left fist landing on his chin. DeMarcus followed with a right hook and Tony fell backwards. The dance floor cleared out around us and like a pack of wolves, Tony's friends swarmed DeMarcus and began to pound him. Instead of folding up, DeMarcus fought back as if he had a point to prove. A second later I was thrown to the floor by the movement of the crowd. By the time I climbed to my feet I saw my cousin and his crew rushing into battle.

I began to scream for help, but none came fast enough and I saw Harold go down after being hit with a barrage of punches. My instincts kicked in and I scrambled for a weapon. I saw a glass on the floor near my feet so I grabbed it and moved toward the rumble. Harold was balled up on the floor as a fat dude kicked him. I made him my target and swung the glass at his face. He didn't see me coming and the glass connected on his face along with my hand. I didn't let it go, banging it into his face a second time.

I hadn't realized it, but the first contact caused the glass to break, making the second contact more of a stabbing. As the jagged edge of the glass hit the fat boy in the eye, blood began to shoot out of his face like a water fountain. Suddenly, like an elephant hit with a poison dart, he collapsed to the floor.

I was in a frenzied mode as I attacked a second man. When the glass sliced him on the back of his neck he stopped his attack and tried to find out what had happened to him. What had happened would require thirty stitches.

Only one guy still fought Harold who was slowly trying to get off the floor. A moment later, the security guards were on there breaking it up. I looked over and to my surprise DeMarcus had held his own and was giving Tony a beating.

Not asking who started it, the mountain sized men with the T-shirts and flashlights were escorting everyone involved out the door. I was looking for my girls when one of the guards grabbed me by my arm and nearly tore it out of socket, "You have to go."

"What?"

He didn't repeat himself as he pulled me to the door. The next thing I knew, there I was on the steps at the front door. "Daaaayyyyuuuuummmm," somebody said pointing at my shirt. I hadn't realized that I'd cut my hand as well. I was wiping the blood on my shirt and pants, waiting for it to clot and stop dripping from my palm.

I looked down and saw a river of blood on my midsection and on my jeans. It startled me to see so much blood. Not because it was coming from me, but because I was sure I looked like an axe murderer. The doors swung open and I saw Harold, DeMarcus and one of their friends get pushed out the door.

"You okay?" I asked Harold. His eye was swelling and his mouth was bleeding.

"Yeah, yeah, I'm tight," he lied. They had fucked him up. But not DeMarcus. He looked like he was ready to go another five rounds.

"You all need to leave the premises." I looked up to see a PG County officer. "Unless you want to take a ride with us."

"Come on, ya'll. Before we get brutalized by PG's finest. Ya'll know how them mutherfuckas be pressed to beat somebody's ass and lie on you," DeMarcus said loud enough for them to hear.

He was a gangsta and I didn't even know it. The door opened again and Brandy, Shante, and Neek stepped out the door. "I was about to leave ya'll bitches." Harold and DeMarcus escorted us to the car.

DeMarcus opened the door for me. "DeMarcus, call me when you get in."

"I will," he gave me a hug.

"Take Harold to the hospital."

"I was thinking that I might need to do that. And what about your hand?"

I grabbed a small towel from the trunk and wrapped it up. "It should be okay."

We hugged and parted ways. We piled into the car and started the engine. "That shit was crazy," Brandy said. "Yo, that nigga DeMarcus was handlin' them niggas."

"DeMarcus? Did ya'll see my girl," Neek screamed out. "She went Freddy Krueger on them niggas. Your ass is the female Rambo," she laughed. "You laid that big nigga out."

"I don't know, ya'll know Tony ass is crazy. You might shoulda left that shit alone," Shante added her opinion.

"Fuck Tony. DeMarcus whipped his ass, and you know he don't want it with Ali," I said.

"I'm just saying," she said.

"Bitch, you ain't *saying* shit…" I barked.

We pulled out the lot and pulled up the street and stopped at the gas station. My hand was starting to hurt like hell so I asked Neek to pump the gas for me. I put ten dollars in and prepared to hop back in the car. "Hey, you want me to drive?" Neek asked. "I'll be careful."

I opened and closed my fist a couple of times. I wasn't sure I could trust her driving skills, but even with the towel wrapped around it, the pressure was killing me. I could tell she really wanted to drive, and since my hand was throbbing I said, "Yeah, okay." I climbed in the passenger's seat. As I watched her adjust the seat and mirror I asked, "Where the hell was Ivan's ass? You know Tony wouldn't act like that if Ivan was here."

"Yeah, my man went down to Atlanta for a summer program at Morehouse. He won't be back until next Friday."

"Oh yeah, you told me that. So he's going to school down south?" we pulled out onto Allentown Road and headed for Suitland Parkway, stopping at the light.

"Not necessarily, he likes the south a lot though. That shit will be hard when he leaves me." Neek lit up when she talked about Ivan. It was heartwarming and I smiled. But when I saw the sparks light up behind her from the next car, my smile disappeared as my heart dropped. I wanted to scream out but I was in shock as four shots were fired from the car in the next lane. Neek never saw them coming. As my glass shattered, I never even ducked.

The car sped off, tires screeching. Bullets intended for me had hit my best friend in the side of her face. I felt the blood and brain matter on my face as Neek was left slumped on the dashboard.

Her foot eased off of the brakes and the car drifted a few feet into the median. Brandy was in the back screaming and Shante looked as though she was about to have a heart attack.

"Is she dead? Is she dead?" Brandy asked.

I didn't answer her. As if Neek and I had shared one heartbeat, I felt her spirit the second it left her body. I leaned over and hugged her tight as I tried to wish her back to life.

Bumping Em'
Chapter 5

A week after Neek's funeral, I moved in with my mother and Dean. Even though I could barely stand to look at either of them, I was actually scared for my life. It didn't take much of a reason or excuse to get Brandy's mother to allow her to spend the rest of the summer with me out in the suburbs. We were all broken up. Even though she routinely tested my nerves, I invited Shante to come and spend a few days with me.

Dean had purchased a home in the community of Lake Arbor out in Largo, Maryland. My mother, trying to reel me back into her life, continued to let me do whatever I wanted. I moved into a room in the basement that had a bathroom with a shower in it. As far as living arrangements went, it was perfect. A week after I moved in, Ali brought a guy over while my mother and Dean were at work. He disconnected the alarm sensor from the back door. I could tip out the back door without having to turn the alarm off. As long as I moved quietly, I could come and go without so much as a chime.

My bouts of depression had everyone worried, but especially my man. Ali had tried to do everything in his power to make it up to me. He kept trying to buy me things, but one night as we rode out to Baltimore Harbor, I told him plain out. "I want Tony, dead."

"Are you willing to kill him?" he asked. "Do you think you could pull the trigger if I brought him to you?"

I thought about the question. In my mind I envisioned Ali pulling up with Tony in the trunk of a car and saying,

'Here he is.' The thought sent my adrenalin racing through my body. I got excited.

Then I blurted out, "Yeah. I'd kill him. No doubt. I wouldn't want to get caught though."

"But what if you did? Would it still be worth it to you? Would you do time if it meant you could take him out?"

I paused for only a minute. "Yeah, I would."

"You'd do twenty years? You want his life that bad?"

"Yeah," I said without hesitation.

"Alright then," he said. "Let's never talk about this again. To anybody."

"Okay." I was content. Something in his voice told me that he was going to handle it."

Brandy, Shante and I were sitting in the backyard, smoking blunt after blunt of the chronic. It was a little after twelve on a sweltering August night. The only light was coming from inside of the pool where we all had our feet in the water. As I watched the ripples of water flowing from our feet, I noticed our three reflections. There were supposed to be four.

"I still can't believe she's gone," I said.

"She's gone to a better place," Shante said.

"You believe that?" Brandy asked.

"I guess."

"I don't," I said. "What could be better than here with her girls? She was only sixteen," I coughed and passed the weed to Shante.

"Yeah, you got a point," Shante said.

"I love ya'll, but you know Neek was like my sister. She was more than a best friend."

"We know. It's cool. But that don't stop us from being here for you," Brandy said. When Shante passed her the weed she took a nice drag and asked, "You know something?"

"What?"

She looked into my face and smiled. "Never mind."

"What, bitch?"

She shook her head 'no' and repeated herself, "Never mind. I'll tell you later, maybe."

"You's a silly ass chick," I shot back.

"I second that," Shante said. "Fuck this. That water looks too good." Before I knew it she stood up and pulled her T-shirt off and stripped down to her panties and jumped into the pool.

"Don't drown with your high ass," Brandy cried out.

Shante was actually a good swimmer. She'd been swimming every chance she had since coming to my house. It was like she was on a mission. I'd noticed how tight her body was getting. Her breasts were a little smaller than mine, but shaped like two perfect softballs. She had a bubble butt and her hips were a little wider than mine.

I watched as she swam like a fish up to the other end of the pool and back. When she made it back to the deep end where we were seated she climbed out and took her spot next to me again, titties out as if we were at a topless beach. "I see someone's mighty proud," Brandy said.

"Well, I ain't ashamed," she slashed back.

"Oh, I ain't either," Brandy returned and was greeted with a smirk and a laugh from Shante.

"Okay, bitch." Then Pocahontas stood up and stripped completely naked. She gave a twirl. It was the first time I'd seen her naked and I was surprised that she had done that. She dove in and shocked the hell out of us. As she swam, I couldn't get the image that I'd just seen out of my head. Brandy's nipples were like erasers. She had a body like a model to match her face. I was hoping like hell that my mother, nor Dean got up for a late night snack and happened to take a peep outside.

I continued smoking until I was completely smashed and then I was too afraid to get in the water. I kept imagining that Jaws was going to somehow appear in the pool and chomp the shit out of us.

An hour later Shante had fallen into a deep sleep on my bed, snoring like an old man. Still high as hell, I showered and then went out to the recreation room to watch television as I dried off and put on lotion. Brandy showered after me and came out to join me while I sat watching *Roseanne* on Nick at Nite.

"It's bad for your eyes, watching TV in the dark like this," Brandy said.

"I know, but I do it all the time. I was just going to do it long enough to put some lotion on but I haven't been able to move." I smiled and added, "I'm too fucking high."

Brandy reached for the lotion and said, "Put your leg here."

She squeezed a handful of Jergens and started to rub it on my leg. Instantly she released tension in my calf muscles that I didn't even know I had. "Mmmm, that feels good, girl."

She stood up and dropped the towel that she had and spread in on the floor. "Lay on this and I'll hook you up with a massage while I do this."

She didn't have to ask me twice. I laid flat on my belly and she went to work, rubbing on my calves and thighs. It felt so good that I think I began to drift off. She moved up to my shoulders and kneaded them with her fingers and knuckles. When she reached my lower back I think I drifted off for a few seconds. Next she startled me when her lotion filled hands landed on my ass. Then she said, "I know this feels good. I love when I get a massage on my cheeks. You get so much tension there that needs to be released. You feel it?"

I did. It felt great. She used two hands at a time on each ass cheek. It was incredible, the amount of tension and relief that she was now using to relieve me of my senses. I truly didn't care that one of my best friends was now rubbing on my derrière. I allowed myself to focus solely on the pleasure until she crossed the line and let one of her fingers slide down and brush against my pussy.

I jumped and said, "What the fuck are you doing?"

"I'm sorry," she said. "That was an accident."

I locked eyes with her. "Was it really?" She didn't answer. I stared at her and asked her flat out, "Brandy, are you gay?"

She was quiet for a second then said, "No, I'm not, but … I do…"

"But what? Either you are, or you aren't."

"It's not that simple. I get turned on by boys and girls. Sometimes when I see sexy women on television, or beautiful strangers, I feel something stirring deep down inside that I really can't explain. I usually can control it, but with you, and my seeing you all the time, it drives me crazy," she answered. "Truthfully, I don't even think I'm gay, because I am really attracted to men, but there's something about you."

I didn't know what to say. It was weird as hell for me to hear it. "How long have you felt like that?"

"I don't know. Maybe the last couple of years. But please, don't let me freak you out. I still love you like a sister."

I smirked, "A sister whose pussy you want to plunge your fingers into?"

She chuckled without shame. "It's just that I've had a fantasy about being with you, eating you out. I don't know why, but I have. I'm sorry… I hope that…"

I was stunned but my mind raced at a thousand miles an hour. As I stared at her naked body, nipples fully erect, her flawless skin and beautiful face, something came over me and I said, "Fuck it." I leaned back on my elbows and spread my legs. "Go ahead, but I'm not doing you back." I couldn't believe I'd said it. Her face showed her disbelief. I tapped my pussy and said, "Hurry up before I change my mind."

As if someone had shot off a starter pistol, she moved in like a tiger and began licking my pussy from the bottom to the top. The warmth of her tongue caught me off guard, as did her delicate touch. Until that moment, I'd believed that Ali had mastered my body and every facet of sex, leaving no room for improvement.

As Brandy used her tongue to launch me to the stratosphere, I lost all regards for the boundaries of what I'd believed was right or wrong. How could having one of my best friends eating me be wrong when it felt so good? Her saliva and my juices were combining to form a small stream that was falling out of me.

It surprised me that Brandy knew exactly where to lick as she gave my clit a sensory overload. Brandy was tickling my love button so that I thought my head was going to pop off. As the connection of her lips and tongue built me up to the point where my stomach muscles grew tight, she was in complete control. I was breathing heavily, trying not to yell out. I reached for the towel that was nearby and covered my face before I screamed loud enough to wake the dead.

She was giving me the sweetest torture I'd ever experienced. Instead of letting me go over the top right then and there she slowed down on her tongue thrashing enough to bring her fingers into the act. She used three of them to massage my pussy from the inside. There were spots inside of me that she found that sent bolts of electricity up my spine. I began to shiver from the pleasure. My clit felt as big as a marshmallow and my pussy was now wet and wide enough for two dicks.

Brandy obviously knew this and without warning, she shoved her entire fist into my pussy.

"Ahhhhhhhyyyyyeeeeeeee," I yelled out as the sparks turned into an explosion. Her mouth was on my pussy like a soldier jumping on a grenade to save his comrades. She locked her mouth onto my mound and rode my pussy through a bronco-style, body-bucking, orgasm. I arched my back as I shook as if I was having a seizure.

My climax was hard, fast and more intense than anything I'd ever felt. When I finished I couldn't move. While I was trying to catch my breath, she spun around, lifted my leg over hers, and the next thing I knew she had her pussy pressed against mine, grinding as if her life depended on it.

It felt okay, but I was too spent to do anything to help her along. I didn't need to. Thirty seconds later Brandy let out a series of small screams, "Ahhhh, ahhhhhh, uhhhhhhhhh, I'm coming, Nia. Uhhhhhh," she groaned.

It was nine o'clock in the morning when Shante woke us. "Ain't ya'll bitches cute." We'd fallen asleep on the floor together, naked, like old lovers. "Get your gay asses up," she laughed not having a clue that she was actually on to something.

I sat up and looked at Brandy who hadn't moved. "Damn, what time is it?"

"Nine, but if we are going to get our hair done, we need to be at Rona's shop by ten."

We got up, dressed, and headed out. Brandy and I hardly said a word to one another the entire day. I didn't want to tell her how good she'd made me feel. I was a little ashamed that I'd enjoyed it so much. I was concerned that we would have sexual tension between us. Most of all I was worried that when she came for more, I wouldn't be able to say 'no'.

Just Drifting

Chapter 6

A week after the school year started, I was walking out of Footlocker in Union Station and I actually bumped right into *him*. It was strange because the second I saw his eyes, I felt Neek's presence.

"Ivan, hey."

"Hey, Nia." He hugged me. I looked down at the little girl holding his hand. Her caramel complexion and wide mouth had me thinking she was his seed. "Who's the munchkin?" I asked.

"This is my niece, Damani."

"She's cute. How old is she?"

He looked down and said, "Tell Nia how old you are."

She held up two fingers and said, "Fwree."

Ivan and I both laughed, "She just turned three. We are going to have to work on getting the right amount of fingers up. I'm about to pick her up a pair of shoes."

"That's nice." I hadn't seen him since Neek's funeral and I think we both had a lot to say but didn't know where to start. I knew that he really cared about her. He was her first and only but his best friend had killed her and now here we were. Both trying not to talk about it. "So how did your college tour go?"

"It was going good... until the whole thing that happened..." he paused. "You know...with Neek."

"With her murder," I helped him. His expression went ice cold.

"Yeah," his voice cracked.

"Well, I know she would want you to press on with that. She was really proud of all the things you were doing." He nodded. There was an awkward silence. I could tell he wanted to say something but he held back. I couldn't take it any longer so I said, "Hey, look. I'ma let you run and I'll catch up with you."

"Yeah, okay," he shot back.

I began to walk off and he called me, "Hey, Nia."

"Yeah, what's up?" I turned back to see his eyes looking as if they were about to tear up. He looked as if he was fighting back some emotion.

"Nia, if you ever want to talk," he cleared his throat, "We should stay in touch."

I paused and thought about his words, trying to decide whether or not I secretly hated him for even knowing Tony. As clearly as I could see him in front of me, I knew that he *was* good. For that reason alone, I couldn't hate him, even though a part of me did blame him. I reached into my purse and pulled out a pen and a piece of paper. "That'll be cool. And you can call me, if *you* ever need to talk. I know you're hurting too."

"More than anybody knows," he said as he stared into my eyes.

"I understand," I said softly and sped off on my way.

A week after seeing him in the mall Ivan called me but caught me in the middle of one of my routine fuck sessions with Ali. Needless to say, I didn't answer the phone and he didn't call back.

Once school started I spent nearly every free moment I had with Ali, or I was back in the city hanging with Brandi and Shante. Every time I thought about reaching out to Ivan something came up and it turned out that I never got around to calling him back.

Ali had a voracious sexual appetite that hadn't begun to let up. All he did was play the streets all day and keep me on my back all night long. It had been four months and his interest in me was as strong as ever. In fact, I was beginning to believe that he was in love with me.

After Tony had shot the Acura up, he'd taken it back out to the dealer and traded it in for a black BMW 325i. He said he didn't want to take any chances on Tony knowing what I was driving. Even though Tony had been out of sight for a couple of months, I had a feeling that it was only a matter of time before Ali would catch up with him. My rage had not subsided at all. I wanted Tony to die, or at least to do a hundred years for what he'd done to Neek.

Being out in the suburbs kept me away from some of the action that I'd grown up around and I began to wonder if I needed to make some new friends at my new school. Brandy's role in my life had changed. Twice after the first encounter, I'd allowed her to go down on me after getting high. Slowly, I began to lose some of what I felt for her as a friend and started to look at her as simply a sex toy. Only for the facts that one: we'd had a long history together and two; Shante was in the dark about our sexual involvement, did I still try to keep a sense of normalcy. The truth of the matter was, I was ashamed of what we'd done and I stopped wanting to be around Brandy as much. If it wasn't for the fact that she gave me such intense orgasms, I might have started to avoid her.

I was now going to Largo High School, which was a change of pace from the schools in the city. Maryland, specifically P.G. County, was like an extension of the District of Columbia, yet the schools, like the neighborhoods, were like night and day. Anacostia, where I'd attended my freshman and sophomore years, was sixty years old at the time. Like so many of the schools in the city, Anacostia High was at the mercy of a city council that couldn't seem to find a way to take care of the serious work that it needed. Largo, which was an air conditioned building with spotless halls, full of happy, well-to-do black kids, seemed more like a college facility to me.

I quickly adapted to the relaxed atmosphere there and the fact that without even trying, I had become a celebrity in the school. The facts that I wore the flyest clothes and was blessed with both a pretty face and a banging body made me stand out, even amongst the spoiled rich kids that attended Largo. This was saying a lot because since the early eighties Largo had been known as the school that housed Prince George's County's cutest girls.

It also amazed me that some of the students had heard about me fighting and taking out two niggas in the club over the summer. I would have never figured out how the word had traveled like that until the day I saw a familiar-looking, fat guy with a patch on his eye walking out of the cafeteria. My heart began to race as I recognized him as the one who I had smashed in the eye with the glass.

He looked right into my face with his one good eye and I knew that he recognized me. He started toward me and I took off running for the side exit. I didn't stop until I reached the student parking lot but panicked when I didn't see my car. Then I realized that I'd been looking in the section where I'd parked the day before. I then turned and sprinted to my car, squeezing the alarm as soon as I was within thirty feet.

I climbed in and started the car and yanked it into reverse only to slam on brakes when an army green station wagon pulled up behind my car blocking me in. My fears were confirmed when the patch-eyed driver emerged and walked up to my window.

I looked around and my heart sank when I realized that there wasn't a soul within a hundred yards. I cracked my window, "Leave me the fuck alone. My boyfriend will kill you if you do anything to me."

"Nia, I'm not going to do anything to you."

"Well move your fucking car. I want to leave."

"I can't do that. Not until you hear me out."

My heart was beating. "What do you want?"

"Listen, I've known you were at this school for the past month. One of my boys pointed you out because he was checking you out. A day later he told me who you were. Everybody knows you are the new chick from the city."

"So what."

He was calm and surprisingly comforting as he spoke. "I just want you to know that I don't have a beef with you. I don't want to be involved in whatever is going on with you and Tony."

"Yeah okay, whatever you say. Can you move your car please?"

He shook his head and a distressed look was on his face. "You don't believe me, but I want to show you something." He walked to his car and brought back his notebook. He opened it and pulled out six pieces of paper. I scanned over the letterhead and saw the names of prominent schools like Florida State, Penn State and Virginia Tech across the tops of the first few. "All these are letters from colleges for me to play football. See, I started for the varsity team here and made All-Met last year in the tenth-grade. I have a chance to go to college and hopefully the NFL, but I can't play this year because of the glass you hit me with. The doctors said that one centimeter lower and I would have lost my eye. Luckily for me, it'll heal completely over the next five months they said."

"Well you shouldn't have been…"

He cut me off, "Nia, I know. You were protecting your family and I understand that now. But I was protecting mine. Tony is my cousin." When he said that, a chill ran down my spine. "But… that nigga is a hothead and fooling with him, I almost lost my entire future. Plus, he had no reason to start that fight." He reached for his letters. "I haven't heard from him since that night. He didn't call to ask if I was okay, say 'my bad' or nothing. So fuck him as far as I'm concerned. I hear that the police are looking for him. My parents don't want me near him and now I see why. Just because somebody has the same blood as you, don't make them family. So I want you to know that I'm not into all this beefing."

I was silent as I listened to what he had to say. He finished with, "I just wanted to let you know that so that you don't have to feel uneasy here at school. And from the way things went down at the club, hopefully I won't have to feel uneasy myself. Plus, I've heard about the guy Ali, and I don't want to have to be looking over my shoulder."

He was referring to Ali's rep as a killer. "I don't even know your name."

"Sheldon Parker."

"Well, Sheldon, it's all good. As long as you don't beef with me, I won't beef with you or tell Ali a thing. I'm just trying to go to school and get my education." He smiled as if he was more relieved than I was. "So what position you play?"

"Defensive end."

I nodded. "Well, I'm sorry about your eye too."

He nodded back and the conversation ended. He pulled off and I did the same after looking at the clock. Still a little drained from the whole rush, I reached into my glove and pulled out some smoke to light up as I set off to take a ride to clear my head. I wasn't in the mood for Ali's intensity right then and knew if I called him he'd have me in a hotel within the hour. I hit the beltway and headed south until I reached Indian Head Highway. I tossed the weed out of the window as I turned onto Old Fort Road.

I pulled into the parking lot of Friendly High School as the half-day students were preparing to leave school. I circled the lot looking for my cousin Harold. I was going to see if he wanted to go catch a movie and hang out. *Seven*, starring Morgan Freeman and Brad Pitt, had just come out and I wanted to check it out.

As I drove around for the third time looking for my aunt's Nissan, I saw none other than DeMarcus walking through the parking lot. I pulled up on him and the girl he was walking with. I looked her up and down, deciding that she was alright *if* he liked tackheads. I frowned at her lack of fashion sense and wondered what she was doing with a honey like my DeMarcus.

"Hey, stranger," I said as I slid my widow down. He hadn't seen me in the BMW but when he recognized me, the look in his eyes gave away his feelings.

"Hey, Nia. What you doing here?"

The girl was staring so I decided to crush her. I climbed out of the car revealing the painted-on, Parasuco Jeans I was wearing and the breast-hugging, Arden B, T-Shirt. I gave him a hug, pressing my fluffy breast into his chest. "I was looking for Harold. Have you seen him?"

"Harold hasn't been to school since Wednesday. He's sick. That's why I'm getting a ride home with my friend Carmen."

"Oh, well, I'll give you a ride. I've been wanting to catch up with you anyway."

He looked nervous but it was a no-brainer. "Carmen already missed her lunch to run me…"

"Well now she don't have to. Come on."

He looked over at Carmen who hadn't said a word. She stood there looking like the assistant librarian or the math club president. "Carmen, I'ma go ahead…"

He didn't finish before she turned and stormed off. I got into the car and he walked around to the other side. When he sat down he had a stupid look on his face. I pulled off, "I know you aren't messing with that geeky bitch, DeMarcus."

"Hell no," he said. "But she's a friend. I've known her for years."

"Yeah, well that bitch desperately wants some dick from you," I laughed. He shook his head as he smiled trying to look comfortable. "So is something wrong?"

"No, it's just that you seem like you've changed. I mean you popping up in different whips. I smell the weed on you. And I don't want to go into the last time we saw each other." He looked me up and down then added, "For real, I should be asking you if there's anything wrong with you."

We pulled out onto the main highway and I asked, "It's a sunny Friday. What do you have planned for the rest of the day?"

He shrugged his shoulders. "Nothing really. I was going to go check on Harold, maybe hit the skating rink tonight."

"Well, I've got plans for the day. I never got to thank you for what you did that night."

"You don't have to."

"But I'm going to," I said as I blasted my favorite Xscape tune, *Who Can I Run To* and pushed the gas pedal taking the car to over eighty miles an hour. "Let's start with a movie, some popcorn…" I reached and grabbed his dick before adding, "…and maybe a hot dog." I laughed even though he looked embarrassed.

I could tell that DeMarcus' mind was being blown. He'd wanted to see *Seven* as well, but we'd both have to see it a second time if we were ever going to figure out what was going on in the movie.

Twenty minutes into the movie and I had his dick in my hand stroking it. Though this was the premier date, it didn't matter because we'd come to a one o'clock show while mostly everyone was still at work. There were only ten other people in the theater and we had the back four rows to ourselves. We'd taken the corner at my direction and now he understood why.

I didn't plan to tease him for long. In fact, I'd visualized my assault on him the entire ride into Waldorf. Now I was well into the second phase as I leaned over and took his dick into my mouth. It was warm and smooth, and I wanted to hit him off with some head that he'd never forget.

I started sucking the tip as I let excess saliva drip from my mouth coating his shaft as I began to jerk it with my hand. "Ohhhhhh," he groaned out. His movements were erratic as if he was fighting to keep control. This was different from Ali, who always maintained control over himself and me. Inside, I was filled with pride as I felt my control over DeMarcus increasing with each suck and stroke of my hand.

"Mmmmmm," I purred as I continued on tickling his meat with my tonsils.

I felt trimmers in him. Ali had taught me how to suck him off to perfection and now what I was doing to DeMarcus wasn't even fair. I shifted gears and started jerking his soaked dick with my right hand, "Shit," he cried out and I felt him begin to pulsate. I pulled my mouth away just in time as he began to squirt gobs of sticky cum into the air. I kept jerking and he whined like a bitch. "Ahhhhhhh, ahhhhhhhh," until he couldn't take another touch and pulled away.

I handed him napkins as he breathed heavily for a full minute more.

As we watched the gore on the screen for the next twenty minutes, he kept an inappropriately bright smile on his face. It was funny because as people were suffering dismemberment and bloody torture on the screen, he looked like a seven-year-old watching an episode of Barney.

Once the glassy look wore off and he came out of the blow job-induced haze he was in, I reached for his hand and stuck it into my panties. I guided him as I showed him how to massage my clit. Giving him long enough to recover, I reached for his dick and found it hard once again. Turned on by the fact that we were getting so freaky in the back of the theater I couldn't take it any more. Before I came, I slid my jeans and panties off of one leg and told him to slide down a bit in the seat.

No where near Ali's size, he felt perfect as I impaled myself on him and began to bounce slowly up and down on him. Knowing that we wouldn't have forever, I began to grind on his lap and started to rub my pussy lips ferociously.

"Come on, boy. Fuck me," I said in a seductive whisper.

"Oh yeah, Nia."

"Work that dick, Dee, work it."

He was humping me as best he could and it was plenty good enough. My pussy was waterfall central, and I knew that if I could see his dick in the darkness, it would be a creamy mess. We fucked in a steady rhythm until I felt the familiar tingle.

"Ayyyyyyyy, yeaaaahhhhhhhh," I screamed out.

People surely heard us. He quickly covered my mouth but as my climax sent me into a zone, I bit down on his fingers and I nutted all over his dick.

I was still panting when the beam from the flashlights hit us. The ushers were standing there, along with a manager. We were caught and we were escorted out of the theater. Once we were back out into the sunlight, I nearly collapsed on the floor laughing. While DeMarcus tried to steady himself from the embarrassment, I learned something about myself.

I simply didn't give a fuck.

Hot Rocks
Chapter 7

I couldn't stop laughing at DeMarcus. He could barely walk after we rode the Shock Wave at King's Dominion. "I told you I don't like roller coasters," he said as he held on to the fence, trying to steady himself. "I know you don't think this is funny," he said.

Even though his face didn't look good, I had never seen anyone who couldn't handle a roller coaster, so when he vomited over the rail I was in shock. I got him some water and we started towards the front gate to make our exit. "Do you want me to see if I can borrow a wheelbarrow?" I joked.

"Real funny," he shot back. "I'ma get your ass back when we get home," he threatened.

By the time we made it to my car he seemed as though he was feeling much better. We stopped at the Tiger Mart and he bought some pills for motion sickness. I hoped he wouldn't let the vomit-filled ending ruin the incredible day that we'd had. We'd ridden the water rides, played a ton of games and even made a video lip-syncing to Biggie's *One More Chance*.

After being thrown out of the movies a week earlier, I'd come up with one excuse after another for Ali so that I could continue spending all of my free time with DeMarcus. I lied to Ali and told him that I was being tutored and trying out for cheerleading. He was always so busy in the streets that he didn't pay it much attention. As long as he could squeeze in a late night booty call, he was fine for the time being.

It was strange because I missed Ali and I definitely didn't want to lose him, but what I was doing with DeMarcus felt fulfilling in a deeper way. It was as if I was completing some sort of unfinished mission. He had been my first and yet I'd never even had a chance to date him. We'd never sat on the phone all night, wrote love letters, or snuck off together. It was a lot like I was suddenly granted a chance to relive a lost moment.

I'd always heard that a woman falls in love with her first. I guess because of the trauma I faced that day, I'd been immune to the love bug. Even now I couldn't deny feeling something special for him, but somewhere the equation had gotten screwed up. As DeMarcus and I humped like rabbits in his basement he said the words, "I love you."

In the afterglow I sat quiet, wondering if he was going to start in with it. It didn't take a minute. "Nia," he said. "I'm in love with you."

I smiled and then I covered my mouth. "What makes you think that?"

"I've never felt like this. I can't stop thinking about you. In school, all day, at night. I want to be with you every minute. I feel like I'm going crazy. I don't even want to look at another girl."

"Wow."

"That's all you have to say? You don't feel the same way?"

I didn't want to lie. "DeMarcus, you know that I have a boyfriend, right?"

"Well you must not care about him very much. Why else would you be over here with me? On the real, how can you even call him that when you've been having non-stop sex with me?"

I didn't want to tell him plainly that I loved sex, so I just said, "It's complicated."

"Well I want you to break up with him."

I paused for a second. "DeMarcus, where do you think I get the money to do all this stuff we do? He keeps the gas in the car that he bought me and he buys me all these clothes. He paid for our trip to King's Dominion."

"I don't care. We don't need that stuff. I'll get a job," he said desperately.

"Listen, we'll talk about this tomorrow," I answered. My phone had been ringing off the hook for the past hour and a half.

"So are you going to go be with him now?"

"DeMarcus, don't start."

"I want to know."

"I'll call you in the morning."

I could see the anger in his eyes. He grabbed my keys and stood up. "You're not leaving."

I calmly put my clothes on and stood up. "DeMarcus, if you don't hand me my keys, you'll never see me or hear from me again." I wanted to see what he was made of.

It actually let me down a little when he handed the keys right over. He was pussy whipped. I hugged him and left.

"Bitch, where the fuck you been all day?" Shante asked.

"I was hanging out with Harold and my family," I replied.

"Well your boy been driving around here every hour looking for you?"

"Who?"

"Tony's bitch ass. I think he's over his boy's house across the way."

"How you know he was looking for me?"

"Well, for one he caught me walking by myself back from the Exxon station and rolled up on me. When I saw it was him, I almost pissed on myself. Then he asked about you. Of course I told him that me and you don't hang out no more since you moved, but I don't think he bought it. He asked me about the Acura.

Then about an hour after that I saw the car he was in come rolling through the parking lot. I just walked out to the dumpster to take some trash out and I saw the car again."

"Listen, I'm going to tell Ali I've been with you today and that we saw Tony. I want you to keep a look out and I'm going to call you back in a minute."

In five minutes I was crossing the Southeast line. I pulled over and dialed Ali's phone number. On the first ring he answered. "Nia, where the fuck you been? I been calling you all day?" he sounded angry as hell.

"I was with Shante…"

"Well why the fuck you ain't answer the phone? You playing games…"

"Listen baby, I had left the phone in my car because we saw Tony and ran in the house. I didn't have time to get it."

His tone changed instantly from angry to heightened alert. "You saw him where?"

"He came around the neighborhood but he didn't recognize my car. Once he pulled off, I ran for the car and left. But Shante told me that he came back and that he's still over there. I think he's at his boy's house."

"What kind of car is he in?"

Oh shit, I thought. I'd forgotten to ask Shante. Immediately I faked a bad connection and hung up on him. I called Shante and got the info I needed.

I re-dialed Ali and when he picked up I asked, "Can you hear me now?"

"I heard you the whole time. Musta been your phone. So what was he driving?"

"A silver Caprice Classic. He might not be in it, but he's parked by the dumpster near building 7417."

"Alright."

"So what you gonna do?" I could no longer hear any response, "Hello?"

He'd hung up without saying goodbye. I wasn't sure why but I continued on towards the scene of the impending crime. I knew I should have been scared but I was more excited than anything. I would never admit to anyone but the thought of seeing violence was strangely becoming a turn on to me.

I pulled over and parked on Fort Davis Street and called Shante letting her know that I was here. Five minutes later I saw Ali drive past me in a burgundy Cherokee with one of his friends. They circled the block and came back a second time. He was so focused on catching Tony that he never noticed my car.

On their second time around they pulled into the parking lot and Ali's friend got out of the truck first. I noticed that he was dressed in all black. It was just after dark and the block was extremely quiet for a Saturday night. I looked up at the sky and noticed the full moon, a perfect night for a murder I thought.

My heart was now pumping twice as fast as normal. I couldn't believe that I had all but ordered a hit on Tony. I felt like the queen of a crime family as I watched the scene unfold.

Ali's friend investigated the car, crouching the whole time. It must have been empty because he stepped away for a second. Next I watched Ali run over and with something wrapped in his hand he smashed the window out of the car, yanked the door open and then the two of them began rifling through the car like police searching for drugs.

They took their time and then they ran back to the Cherokee. My nerves were starting to get the best of me as I wondered what they were doing. I decided to reach for the bag of weed I had in my console. Wanted to smoke just enough to

71

calm my nerves. A moment later I was blowing smoke out of my moon roof, relieving myself of all tension.

I sat there for a good while until I started to get anxious all over again. I called Shante, when she didn't answer I dialed Brandy's number. "What's up girl?"

"Nothing. What you doing? I was just thinking about you. Are you coming to get me?"

"Yeah, we can hang out. As a matter of fact I'm around the corner from you now."

"Yeah, well be careful, Tony's ass been around here lately."

Speak of the devil and the devil appears. I dropped the phone as I heard the unmistakable sound of pistols popping off. I looked over but didn't see where the shots were coming from, but they seemed to go on and on for at least a minute. I wanted desperately to go and investigate, but I didn't want to walk into the middle of shots being fired.

CRACK, CRACK, CRACK, CRACK, another series of shots rang out and then my heart stopped when I saw two police cars turn into the complex. I climbed out of the car and started towards the court yard. Just then I saw Ali and his friend running toward his truck but they were being followed by a police officer playing super cop. Ali's friend reached the other side of the truck and started shooting at the officer.

I ran back to my car as fast as my feet would carry me. I heard a man moan out and I looked back to see Ali's friend go down. Ali took off running down Fort Davis Street headed towards W Street. I started my car and drove after him. I hit my horn and he looked over at me in total shock. I slammed on the brake and he ran to my car.

"Get the fuck out of here," he huffed out. He was sweating and trying to catch his breath. "We also got to get rid of this." He had a gun still in his hand.

He directed me left, right and left again. When we were way clear of the scene he had me pull into Anacostia Park. He ran over to the water and tossed the gun. "I'ma drive now," he said.

He seemed much more calm. Then he said loud and proud, "I lit your boy up." I didn't ask him anything but he went on. "I'll give it to the little bitch. He put up a fight. He was ready for war, but he wasn't no match for your man. This nigga had a fucking bulletproof vest on."

Then as if he'd just remembered. "I can't believe the police shot my man, Kurt. Kurt is a mother fucking soldier. I hope he…"

I interrupted. "There was a lot of shots fired."

"Yeah, he almost had us cornered. It was like he knew we were coming for him. Maybe he did, but it wasn't enough. I dumped five into his face. Kurt hit him a couple of times in the chest before we knew he had a vest on. This shit is going to be all over the news. Just wait.

I threw a half ounce of coke on him to make it look drug related. They barely investigate those murders, but because we shot that bitch and the other dude, it's gonna be big news."

"What bitch?" I asked.

"When we rolled up on him, he was all hugged up on some chick, or at least pretending to be. For a second, I thought it was you from the back, but once we were close enough to bust off, he pushed her to the ground and started blasting. She tried to run off, but I clapped her in the back at least twice I know."

By the time we pulled up to his apartment complex off of Kenilworth Road in Hyattsville, my phone was ringing. We got out to head inside as I answered. I figured Brandi was going to start asking where I was and what was taking so long, instead when I picked up the phone she was screaming and crying hysterically, as she kept repeating my name, "Neeeeeeyaaaaaaaaahhhhhh, oh God. Neeeyaaaaaaaaahhhhhh, Neeeeeeyaaaaaaaaahhhhhh,"

"Calm down, I can't hear you," I begged as I stopped in my tracks. I had an eerie feeling almost predicting what she would say next.

"Shante's... been... shot."

News and Moves

Chapter 8

I sat in front of Ali's television with my eyes glued to the set. A reporter from NBC-4 was on the scene with breaking news. *'Two murdered and two injured. One of the injured, a seventeen year-old senior at Anacostia High School. She is in critical condition and has been rushed to the hospital, no word yet on whether she is expected to survive. The other injured is twenty-four year old, Kurt Watkins of Naylor Road, Southeast. Watkins is believed to have been one of several shooters involved in the murders. He was wounded in an exchange of gunfire with D.C. officers who arrived on the scene as he attempted to escape.'*

Officers still were moving about behind yellow tape as the anchor asked questions about the slain. The reporter went on *'Tony Sharp, eighteen and James "Batman" Rogers, seventeen were pronounced dead at the scene.'* When their pictures flashed on the screen a chill came over me. The guy Batman had been the third guy with Tony the day we'd met him and Ivan.

'Police are seeking at least one other man, Ali Nixon, for questioning. He is not a suspect at this point, but police believe that Watkins was driving a vehicle registered to Nixon.'

I didn't wake my mother when I crept into the house. Ali went in with me as if he didn't trust that I'd come back out. He let me pack a suitcase and trash bag full of my belongings. "I don't know when we coming back," he said.

At two A.M. we hit I-85 on our way down south. Ali was driving listening to Mobb Deep, smoking blunt after blunt. I dozed off and when I woke up we were at a Hardee's drive-thru window in Charlotte, North Carolina. I looked up and wiped my eyes as we were pulling off. He handed me the bag and we headed back toward the interstate.

"Hand me a sandwich. I got one for you too."

I fumbled through the bag and asked, "Which one is yours and which is mine?"

"They all the same. Chicken and egg. Everything else had pork and you know I can't stand the smell of no fucking pork."

Ali's mother was Muslim, and he claimed to have never ingested pork in his entire life. "You're not tired?" I couldn't believe he could smoke weed like that and not be ready to dose off.

"Hell no. Ain't no time to be tired. You understand what's going on back home don't you?"

"The police are looking for you?"

"They looking for *us*." I gave him a puzzled look. He went on to explain, "If your girl don't die, then she done told the police who shot her. She done told them that I'm your man. They going to come looking for you and when your momma find out you missing, she's going to call the police. Them motherfuckers ain't stupid by a long shot. They are going to know you either helped me or planned it. They're also going to know you are on the run with me. So they looking for *us*."

My stomach began to hurt as I wondered what the hell I had gotten myself into. For some reason for the first time in a while I thought about my father and how he was probably feeling at that very moment, being forced to wake up at right about the same time that I was cruising into the deep south.

After he'd eaten half of his food he slipped in R. Kelly's latest CD. He began to bob his head as if he didn't have a care in the world, singing along to the words. *'Can't you see, we were meant to be, ohhh baby, down for each other for eternity,'* came softly off his tongue as he looked over at me. "You see, this man is so fucking deep. That's real. That's how I feel about you, Nia." He reached for my hand. "You and me were meant to be. Please believe, I love them streets back home, but I gave all that up for you. You wanted that nigga dead, so I killed him for you."

The more I listened to him, the more scared I grew. I wasn't fearful that he would harm me, but more so that I was stuck with him. Suddenly I missed DeMarcus and my mother. "We can't go back there, at least not for a good while. I'm *not* going to jail."

"For how long you think? I'll get put out of school."

He laughed. "Put out of school? Is that what you worried about? Nia, do you understand what happened?"

"Yeah but…"

"Nia, I know I pulled the trigger and I'm a man. I made a decision. You didn't make me do it. Tony would have killed you if he ever saw you. I got to give it to him, the lil' nigga finally grew some heart. Plus, he was afraid of me, so he would have tried to kill me eventually. That's how niggas do. A scared nigga will get at you quick. So you could have closed your eyes and tried to wish it away or you could have done something about. He wasn't going away. You found that out. He tried to take your head off, but he got your girl instead. Niggas like him don't stop. It is what it is. This is your life, love it or leave it. We have to bounce and just get low for a while. Maybe a year or two and this shit will blow over. The case will be cold, ya' know, dead in the water. If your girl Shante lives and I find out she's going to testify then I can solve that too, and we can go home soon enough."

I began to cry. I couldn't believe all of the pain that I'd seen in my short life. Now here I was listening to talk about murdering people I'd grown up with so that I could go back home.

Ali rubbed my shoulder and said, "It's okay get it out. Let that shit out."

I tried but the crying made it hard for me to speak. "I'm going... to miss my...mother... and... and... Brandeeeeee," I cried like a baby. "I didn't... mean... for...." I couldn't finish as the snot began to pour out of my nose.

"It'll be okay. You'll love down south. I'll tell you what. I'll get you a new I.D. and you can still finish school, maybe even go to college. Would you want to do that?" I heard him and appreciated him trying to be sweet, but I couldn't stop crying. He pulled over at the next exit. "I'm going go get a room for us. You can take a hot shower and take a nap for a few hours. Plus I need to count my money."

When we got to the room, Ali emptied out a gym bag and counted up two hundred and sixteen thousand dollars. I had never imagined that he had that kind of money. I realized then that the money he gave me was nothing. "I had to leave a lot more behind, but it's in a safe place. But we can still get on our feet with this."

I laid on the bed and tried to close my eyes, but my mind was racing a million miles an hour. I needed to smoke something to help me relax. While Ali was showering, I lit up and took a few puffs.

He walked out of the bathroom soaking wet. I knew what was coming next. I expected to get pounded out by him, but for the first time he was gentle with his sex. He kept kissing me in the mouth and he worked me slow. Keeping one leg up on his shoulders, he grinded me instead of plunging in and out. The friction came, but it felt different. His kisses, mixed with the weed, took me away. I felt myself drifting away on a cloud. "I just want you to feel good," he kept saying.

He didn't know how good I was feeling. His hot ass dick was starting to melt away all of my stress, when he stopped and pulled it out. "What... why..."

"Shhhhh," he said as he slid down my body. "I need to taste you."

As his lips met my pussy I noticed even this was more gentle and passionate. He ate me slowly and deliberately, for a moment reminding me of Brandy's pussy-licking technique. As his tongue swirled around my pussy like a kid eating a soft-serve ice cream cone, I felt the hint of a climax coming. I was in control of it, enjoying the sensations until Ali pulled a new trick out of the bag. He locked down and created a vacuum of suction, lifting my clit up from between my vaginal lips, then, he stuck his index finger into my rectum.

I don't know what happened to my body next as I lost control. I felt as if I pissed on myself as fluid poured out of my pussy. I came so hard that I got a cramp in my feet from pointing my toes out ward. My body was flat as a board as my ass locked around his finger as he continued to eat me through one of the best orgasms ever.

I didn't realize that tears were running down my cheeks. Ali sensed that I couldn't take any more. He moved up to me and held me as we spooned. Never getting back to a fully conscious state, he allowed me to drift off to sleep.

I never asked exactly where we were heading. It wouldn't have mattered because I had never traveled further south than Virginia Beach and wouldn't have had a clue as to where we finally wound up. I did start to notice the signs as we passed through South Carolina and then into Georgia. It was close to midnight when we pulled up to a house in Decatur, ten miles outside of the city of Atlanta.

A skinny brother who reminded me of Jimmy Walker, the one who played J.J. Evans on *Good Times*, answered the door. "Ali, heyyyyy cousin," he said with an embrace.

Ali introduced me to his cousin Ricky. "Nice to meet you," I said.

"Yeah, well welcome to my home. Come on in, let me help you get yourself settled."

We wound up in a room upstairs that had a window A.C. unit. "This is just temporary. I need to make a couple of moves and we'll find a spot real soon. We can't stay in hotels, they are going to be too hot. Plus we have to get rid of your car."

"What?"

"Yeah, those D.C. plates are going to draw attention. In a few days, if not already, they'll be in the system. We get pulled over and it's all over. But I'll get you another one." He smiled and said, "It ain't like you got anywhere to go for a while anyway."

He said it trying to make light of the situation, but I didn't think it was funny. Wasn't a damned thing funny about being a fugitive.

One month later and the boredom was starting to take its' toll on me. Ali hadn't allowed me to leave his sight unless he had a "move to make" and left me. With the life I was living now, I may as well have been locked up. We were still staying with his cousin Ricky and I got tired of him undressing me with his eyes every chance he got. The whole situation was making me sick. I seriously began to contemplate leaving and going home, but everyday Ali seemed to reinforce his hold on me with backbreaking sex and the fear he instilled in me through the horror stories about prison.

He had me convinced that I was going to be buried underneath a jail. Sitting around watching an episode of Jerry Springer where mothers had come on the show fighting pimps to get their daughters back, I decided to pick up Ricky's phone and make a call. I was smart enough to use the call block when I dialed the number.

'You have reached the home of Dean and Vernelle Beverley. We're not home right now so please leave us a message so that we'll know you called.'

"Ma, this is Nia. I just called to let you know I'm okay. I know you've been worried about me, but I'm fine. I just needed to get away for a while. I'll call you …soon."

I had tears in my eyes after I left the message. I hope that it would make her feel better hearing my voice. Once I got myself together I dialed a second number. When she picked up I got nervous and almost hung up on her. "Hello, hello…"

"Brandy, it's me."

"Nia. Omigod. Girl, what is up? Where the hell are you?"

"I can't go into that on the phone, but I just wanted to find out what's been up."

"Nia, I can't believe it's you. I thought your ass might have been dead. After the call dropped that night I told you about Shante and you never called back, I didn't know what to think."

"So how is Shante?"

I could feel her whole tone shift into a more dismal state as she delivered the update. "Shante is in a wheelchair. The doctor's said it's fifty-fifty that she'll walk again. She's had like two surgeries already."

"Damn," I huffed out.

"So what's the word on the street?"

"Everybody was saying that Ali just went crazy and shot everything up. His man Kurt got caught, but he ain't snitch or nothing. So I don't know if the police know what really went down. Have you talked to him?"

"Huh?"

"Have you talked Ali?"

"Oh… no, I haven't."

"So what are you doing? Your mother has been going crazy, driving around here every day after work. I know you were beefing with her but she loves you."

Changing the subject I said, "Hey, if I send you a letter, can you drop it in the mail for me. I wrote my father a letter, but I don't want to send it from here. So I can mail it to you and then you mail it to him."

"Yeah, no problem." We both grew quiet, trying to find something to say. Finally she asked, "Did you have anything thing to do with the killing?"

"What?"

"Some people have been saying you had everybody shot up. They said you was around here and that you drove the getaway car."

"Hell no. That's a lie. Where you get that from?" I lied trying to hide that I was now nervous.

"The police came to my house and asked me if I knew anything about that. If I'd talked to you or knew your whereabouts."

"Well that's some bullshit."

"I just wanted to tell you."

"Thanks," I shot back. More silence and I finally said, "Well, Brandy, I'ma run. I'll call you soon."

"Wait," she said. "I just want you to know... I miss you. I miss you so much. I've never had anyone that I could be myself with and what I had with you... it meant so much."

"I miss you too, B," I said and hung up the phone. With that conversation I realized that I couldn't go home. Ali knew the streets and he had been right.

I picked the phone up and placed my last phone call. I wanted to get some closure, to say goodbye. I was going to be cool but the second I heard his voice I burst into tears, "DeMarcus..." I cried out.

"Nia?"

"I'm sorry," I said.

"Baby, where are you?"

"I wish I had never left you. I'm sorry."

"Nia..." I didn't say anything. He heard my crying. "Nia, I love you."

I hung up the phone.

Love the One You're With

Chapter 9

I was happy as hell when Ali and I finally moved into our own place. It was a two bedroom apartment out in College Park, in Southwest Atlanta. The best thing about moving was the fact that I actually was able to see other people coming and going, having real lives. There were plenty of Atlanta University students in our complex as well as a bunch of other young professional couples. I enjoyed dreaming of the day that I could have a *regular* life like them.

Ali also finally bought another car, a Mazda MPV. He said that driving a minivan helped him keep a low profile. He never got rid of my car, instead he bought a car cover and left it in Ricky's back yard. I missed driving it, but I understood why I couldn't.

We'd been in Atlanta for three months already and I missed home, with spending Christmas without my family being especially hard. But one day at a time, I was beginning to get used to the laid back lifestyle. From the time we moved into our place, all I did was shop, eat and wait for Ali to come home. He had gotten himself plugged into the streets in Atlanta and he seemed happy with the money he was making. While he slept all day, I drove to the malls, Lenox Square, Phipps Plaza and Perimeter Mall, where I spent whatever I wanted. It got to the point where it felt as though shopping was my job.

What was crazy was that I had so many unworn outfits in the closet. I started to feel silly buying clothes, so I stopped. I started buying jewelry and watches instead. Ali would plunk

84

down hundreds in ones, fives and tens, telling me to get rid of it. I had no problem.

Early in January I sat in the bed watching Fox news as they were talking about the huge 'Blizzard of 96' that had just finished dumping record snow on the entire Northeast. Some parts of the D.C. area had gotten up to three feet of snow. I was thrilled that I wasn't at home to deal with it. Remembering what it was like to be stuck in the house gave me a new appreciation for the Georgia climate. As I watched highlights of cars stuck in the snow and downed power lines, I finally became content with my living arrangements.

Most students were just going back after missing a week of school. I remembered the days when a day out of class seemed like hitting the lottery. Now that seemed like such a long time ago.

I needed to hear from someone back home, so I dialed Brandy's number. When a voice much deeper than hers answered I was a little shocked, "Hull-o," the person said.

"Yeah, hello, is Brandy there?"

"Who is this?"

I wasn't about to respond to the nosey person who had no phone manners. I repeated myself. "Is Brandy there? Is this Brandy's phone?"

"Yeah, it's Brandy's fucking phone but like I said, I want to know who this is?"

I laughed, "Man, stop playing with me."

Next I heard Brandy in the background starting to yell. "Gimme my fucking phone." I could tell there was a struggle and I wondered why. It should have been clear to the person on the phone that it was a woman on the other line.

The phone sounded as if it hit the floor and I heard Brandy yelling, "Get the hell out." Then after scrambling for the phone, my homegirl picked the phone up. "Yeah, who dis?"

"Bitch, is that how you answer the phone now?"

"Ohhhhhh shit, Nia. What's up girl?" she started rambling on trying to get out a thousand words in the first sentence. *When was I coming home, where was I, what was I doing?* It was so good to hear her voice.

"Who the hell was that fool answering your phone?"

She exhaled, "Please, don't even make me go there right now. Tell me about *you*."

I wanted to tell her everything I was doing but I couldn't. Instead I told her that I had left because I was afraid of Ali and the whole thing with my father had just been too much on me. I sold her a story that I'd needed a change of pace.

As we talked she said, "I have to tell you something that you'll never believe."

"What's that?"

"Guess who I ride the bus with to school? I mean... that is *when* I go... and hang out with him all the time?"

"Who?"

"Jasper."

"Bucktoothed Jasper, who lives in my old apartment?"

"Yeah, your cousin."

"You know that fool ain't none of my cousin. You ain't never seen no funny looking people in the Morgan family," I cracked up laughing.

"Believe it or not, Jasper is coming into his own. He's cool once you get to know him. I just don't think anyone has ever given him a chance."

"Well more power to you. What do you two possibly have to talk about?"

"We got a lot in common. You can't judge a book..."

"Whatever."

As we sat on the phone the conversation began to get a little more serious. Shante was still in a wheel chair. It didn't look good for her. She also shared some new dirt that came as a shock to me. "Shante was fucking with Tony. I didn't know until after she got shot. I spent a lot of time at her house once she came home from the hospital trying to give her moms some help. One day while Shante was sleeping, her moms was feeling all emotional and started crying about how her baby's life was ruined over a dirty, little, nigga. During the conversation, her mother told me she'd been running around with him for a while. I guess she didn't know the history behind it, or that it was supposed to be a secret. For real, I don't even know where she met him. I guess she had plenty of chances since the nigga was always in the neighborhood."

"I'm not surprised. That bitch has always been jealous of me."

"Well, I'm sorry about that. I don't like that shit and you know if I'd have known, I woulda' filled you in. What really has me fucked up is that she actually tried to set you up that night."

"How do you know this?"

She got quiet for a second. "She told the police everything. Like that she talked to you right before the shooting."

"So are they looking for me?"

"I don't know if they want to press charges, but they believe you are with Ali and they want him for two murders, soooo…"

My heart sank as this information confirmed to me that I could probably never go home. About thirty minutes later I tried to get off the phone and Brandy came right out and said, "There's something else I need to tell you. I need to tell someone."

"What's up?"

Her voice dropped to a whisper. "I don't know what I've gotten myself into. I need some help." All of a sudden she sounded sullen.

"Go ahead, B. You can tell me anything."

She calmly said, "The person who answered my phone. Her name is Lou."

"*Her*?"

"Yeah. She's my girl… and…" she paused and wouldn't go on.

"And what?"

"She's crazy. I don't want to be with her anymore, but I'm afraid."

"Afraid of what? Has she put her hands on you?"

She went silent again. "Listen, I didn't mean to…"

"Fuck that. Don't be letting no bitch put her hands on you. Where you know her from?"

"I met her around here. She manages the Domino's up the street."

She may not have understood my train of thought but I knew what needed to happen. "Listen, how are you doing in school?"

She laughed in sarcastic way. "I haven't been to school regularly since Shante came home from the hospital in October. I never really got into it from the start. First Neek died, then you left. After I saw Shante in that chair, it was like, fuck it. I go every now and then. I guess you could say I'm taking the year off."

We all were, it seemed. Brandy had less structure than all of us. Her mom's had been on the pipe since 1990 and even though she continued to work at the post office over in Brentwood, she didn't give a damn about Brandy. "Brandy, I'm going to call you tomorrow morning. I want you to be at

88

Rivertowne Plaza by ten A.M. You are going to come with me."

"Come where?"

"Don't worry about that. Just know that when you get here, I got you." I sensed her hesitation. "C'mon B, I really want you to come and keep me company. You can just stay for a little while or as long as you want, but listen…"

"Yeah?"

"None of that sexual shit between us." That scared me, mostly because it blurred the lines for me. I hated myself for enjoying it. I didn't think it was right, plus after getting my pussy licked like that, I needed a dick. A person who can and will take pleasure from anything is but a step above an animal I'd decided. I wasn't gay so I don't care how much weed I smoked, I wasn't going that route again.

She laughed, "That's cool, but are you serious about me coming?" She sounded excited.

"Dead serious. I'll call you tomorrow. Just make sure you are at the plaza and make sure you answer when I call."

I grabbed a wad of cash from the tampon box in the back of my underwear drawer and caught a cab out to Ricky's house once Ali went out to hustle. I pulled the cover off of the car and then, equipped with a bag full of Coca-cola, No-Doz and Doritos I hit the interstate determined to make the trek back into the city unnoticed.

I burned up the highway all night long, only stopping twice to use the bathroom. I felt like a secret agent every time I stopped to get gas. The amazing thing was that I didn't see a single trooper in four states. The further north I traveled I noticed the scenery became all white with snow piled high on the shoulder of the interstate. A little after ten A.M., I crossed the Woodrow Wilson Bridge and headed for Rivertowne Plaza. Once I got there, I went to a pay phone and called Brandy.

Again the deep voice, "Bitch, why you calling my girl."

"Listen you dyke, you put your hands on my girl again, I'm gonna split your shit open."

"Oh yeah," she responded.

"Yeah, if you think it's a game, try me. You must not know who the fuck I am."

"We'll see about that," then she hung up the phone. I was furious.

I climbed back into the car and contemplated my next move as I drove through the plaza. I thought that perhaps Lou had gotten wind of Brandy's plan and was holding her captive. I didn't want to go around Southeast, but I wasn't leaving without Brandy. When I circled past the Old Navy I was shocked when I saw what looked like a scene out of *What's Love Got to Do With It* with Brandy, playing Anna Mae, struggling to get free from Ike.

I sped up and stopped next to them. Brandy saw me and her eyes lit up. She used all of her might to break free and then she took off sprinting across the lot. Lou wanted to take off after her, but slipped on some ice, giving Brandy a good head start as she started dodging off between parked cars trying to get away. I pulled out in front of Lou, blocking her path to give my girl a head start. I was simply going to pull over to where Brandy had run, but Lou was relentless. The big bitch jumped up off the ground and gave chase through the parking lot.

Brandy was at least thirty yards ahead when her scorned lover made it to the lane where she'd run. Not wanting to waste any more time, I made my move. I looked around the lot for security and when I didn't see any police I floored the car right toward them and mowed Lou's ass down. I flinched when I realized how hard I'd hit her.

As Lou screamed out, Brandy turned around to see what I'd done. She shrieked as she saw her girlfriend's leg looking like a broken table. I pulled up next to her. Brandy had a look of displeasure on her face. I was sure she never expected I'd resort to such means, but I didn't have time for her to contemplate my methods. I rolled the window down, "It was either you or her. Get your ass in."

"We can't just leave her there like that."

"B, I don't have time for this, if the police come, I'm going to jail. Now get in." She hesitated and I yelled at the top of my lungs, "GET IN."

This time she jumped and we pulled off. I drove around a huge mountain of snow and headed for the exit. As we drove down Saint Barnabas Road I felt a sense of happiness to have Brandy in my presence, but I also felt overcome with anger when I got a chance to see how this beautiful girl had been battered. She had a knot on her forehead and I could tell that her lip had been busted recently. I couldn't believe she'd let this happen to her.

Still, as anxious as I was to get her back to the ATL, so that I could start helping her get herself together, we had one more stop to make.

Harold and DeMarcus walked out of the side door of the school together after I'd called my cousin letting him know that I was here. We all left Friendly High together and went to DeMarcus' house to chill a while before we hit the road. He lived in the same development as Harold and I was slightly paranoid going anywhere near my family member's homes but I needed at least an hour or two of rest before driving back and I didn't want to sleep at a rest stop.

DeMarcus' lived in a white brick house in a cul-de-sac with its' back to the golf course. With the snow, his home looked like something out of a Norman Rockwell painting. As privileged a life as he lived, it made me wonder where he got the edge to handle himself the way he did and also why he was so into a little hood princess like myself.

We went in and headed downstairs where DeMarcus' bedroom was. Brandy was still a wreck. She obviously was having a hard time dealing with the fact that I nearly turned her lover into road kill. "Get my friend a drink. Something to calm her nerves."

Harold was all too eager to oblige. I knew his motive though. He was hoping that she'd get drunk and become easy. He'd been wanting to fuck Brandy for years, in fact, my cousin would have fucked any of my friends given half a chance. Unfortunately for him, Brandy was in no shape or mood to give up any ass today and to be honest, I didn't even know if she'd even been with a man since the first one.

As for me and *my* man, I didn't think that Harold knew about me and DeMarcus either, but I didn't give a damn. He was about to find out. Big cousin or not, he was going to find out that his best friend was in love with his little cousin. I missed him, loved him and I was about to show him.

Back in Atlanta, I'd left a note for Ali that would slightly squelch the drama before it started. He was going to have a fit when he found out that I'd come back to D.C., but I figured I'd be on the road by the time he even realized I was gone. I knew his habits. He would come in the house at seven or eight A.M., high and tired as hell. He'd turn on Sports Center, while he ate a bowl of Cap'n Crunch, and then fall asleep on the couch like clockwork. He'd wake up around two or three. If I was in the house, he'd want to fuck and eat before he went back out. If his keys weren't on the table in front of him and he was missing a few hundred dollars then he'd assume I was at the mall. Days when I traveled using MARTA, he might not even see me before heading out. I'd learned that it was essential for a woman to learn her man's habits and schedule. Ali was easy because his movements were methodical.

I had another few hours at least before he even wondered where I was. What was strange was that DeMarcus and I didn't get right down to screwing. Instead he wanted to talk. We wound up sitting in the kitchen catching up while he heated up some fried chicken that his mother had prepared the night before. My nerves and my stomach felt better after we chowed down. After we ate he led me into the living room where he let me doze off for an hour. When I woke up we talked for nearly an hour more about our situation. Finally he cut to the chase.

"Nia, tell me the truth. Where have you been?"

Caught off guard by his asking, I said, "Atlanta."

"All the way in Atlanta?" he said as if I'd just mentioned a foreign country. "Why don't you come home and straighten this all out. You didn't do anything."

"It's not that easy."

"I'll be by your side, no matter what."

"If I get sent to jail for twenty years?"

"You won't go to jail for twenty years. You didn't kill anybody," he paused and then came, "Did you?"

"No."

"Well, will you come back?"

"I can't."

"Because of him?"

"No. I'm just scared. You and I both know that the justice system doesn't always work for our people." He went on and on about how my being a minor would keep me from getting into any real trouble and that running from my problems would only make them worse. He made me think about my mother and how she was feeling.

It didn't seem as if he'd let up so I cut him off. "So are you going to make love to me?"

He looked down at the carpet. Then he shocked me with his answer. "No. I can't."

I frowned up and my eyebrows made a V shape showing my displeasure, "What?"

"I've started seeing somebody else." I looked at him as if he was speaking Chinese. "I have a girlfriend and I don't want to cheat on her."

"Who is it? I know it's not that skinny, nerdy, bitch I saw you with that day." His facial expression gave him away. I paused and then asked, "You love *her*?"

Without hesitation, he responded. "I'm not in love with her. But she has been here for me. All the days when I was sad and missing you, she was here as a friend. It just turned into something more."

"What about all that stuff about me coming home?"

"Nia, if you come home, I'll end it with her. But I can't throw away what I have with her if you're going to stay away with another man."

"So it's like that?" He shrugged his shoulders. "She's not even your type." I looked at DeMarcus. He could have been a model. The nigga was handsome enough to melt ice. "*I'm* your type."

"It's not all about looks. You're cute and have a nice body..."

"No, nigga, I'm *pretty* and I have a *great* body."

He shook his head, "Yeah, you have all of that, but that's not why I love you. It's a deeper connection. I feel like GOD put me here to protect you. To save you."

94

"Save me from who? Ain't nobody gonna do nothing to me."

He paused for a second. "Maybe to save you from yourself."

His words touched me. DeMarcus was sincere and I appreciated that he felt so deeply for me, but my mind was on something else. "So you're serious? You're not going to make love to me?"

"No, I'm not."

It was like a slap in the face. I stood up and said, "Fuck this. I'm out." I got up and stormed off. I stopped and when I looked back, he had his face in his hands, looking totally defeated.

I headed to the steps and walked into the basement. It was now dark and when I turned the corner at the bottom of the steps, I stopped in my tracks. I saw Harold's naked back and ass. He had his hands firmly on Brandy's ass as she was sprawled across the pool table.

"Whoooooooooo, yeah, yeah, uhhhh," was all I heard as he was giving Brandy, what looked like a real good fucking.

Harold was grunting as he put work in. I don't know why but I felt a sense of relief that Brandy really did like men, and I was proud that Harold had been smooth enough to finally get himself a piece.

I started back up the stairs, but I stopped when I heard her start to go crazy. I looked back around the corner. Harold had flipped her over and now he'd lifted her up off of the table. He was suspending her. She had her arms around his neck and her legs around his waist as he used her ass cheeks to lift her up and down. He was giving her a ride on his dick as she held on like there was no tomorrow.

In all actuality, there wasn't. I walked back up the steps as I heard her having what sounded like a serious orgasm. I grabbed my coat and looked at DeMarcus. "Tell Brandy that I'm starting the car. I'll be waiting outside for her."

"Nia, come on lets…"

"Thanks for the food," I said and marched out the door through the snow.

Brandy came jogging out the door five minutes later. She climbed in the car, hair mussed, one hundred and fifty percent more relaxed than she'd been when we arrived.

"You ready, bitch," I asked.

"Let's get the hell outta Dodge." She fumbled around with the seat, "How do I recline this seat?"

"Right on the side."

"Oh, I feel it," she said as she found the knob. "Do you mind if I doze off for a little bit?"

"Nah, go ahead."

Five minutes later, she was nearly asleep as we crossed the Woodrow Wilson Bridge headed southbound. I listened to Phyllis Hyman's *When I Give My Love This Time,* mainly because I needed a sad song to go along with the cry that I was secretly having. I wiped my eyes quickly each time a tear rolled down my cheeks.

I decided at that moment that I would forget that DeMarcus ever existed. He could have that ugly bitch. I had Ali. He was paid, handsome and he loved only me. That had to count for something.

If I couldn't be with the one I loved… then fuck it.

In the Trap
Chapter 10

Ali did everything short of punching a hole in me once he found out that I'd gone back home on a mission. He was waiting at Ricky's house when Brandy and I pulled up at one A.M. I'd warned Brandy that it might get ugly but that under no circumstances was she to get involved. Unless of course she thought the nigga was killing me for real.

"How can you say that after you just got on me for letting Lou beat on me?"

"This is different. I did disrespect Ali, and he has done a lot for me. Shit, he supports me. That bitch Lou wasn't splitting her pizza tips with you, was she?"

"Nah."

"I didn't think so."

I took a deep breath as I walked through the door, I was hoping we'd go into our old bedroom. I didn't get past the kitchen. Ali yelled in my face for five or ten minutes demanding that I explain my stupidity. When I'd open my mouth to try, he'd yell, "Shut the fuck up."

Next, he'd squeeze my cheeks with his hands and then yell. I think he was pissed that I didn't cry. "I gave my life up for you. I walked away from an apartment full of furniture and clothes." He didn't know that I'd overheard him coordinating a move with his cousin to pick his things up.

We argued in Ricky's house for almost an hour, which meant he yelled at me non-stop. My body was sore from him yanking me around like a rag doll. I really didn't realize how serious an infraction I'd made until he took the time to break it down for me.

"If the police had caught you and locked your ass up without me, and then threatened to put you in a cell for twenty years, would you have done the dub, or would you have told them where to come pick my black ass up?" Without giving me a chance to answer. "Don't answer that, because I might have to do something to your dumb ass if you say the wrong answer."

Once we made it back to our place he went into the room and slammed the bedroom door. I sat on the couch with Brandy for a little while. I turned the television on for her and once she dozed off I turned the knob to the bedroom door.

I crept up on the bed and touched him to see if he was sleep. He didn't move, so I took my clothes off and slid into the bed next to him.

"Baby, I'm sorry. I just couldn't leave her like that," I'd said humbly, believing he could hear me. I pulled the sheets down and looked at his dick hanging between his legs. I eased down the mattress until it was at my face and I opened my mouth. I wrapped my lips around the head of it and when it began to swell up, I knew that he'd get over his anger pretty quickly.

"Bitch, don't you do no more dumb shit like that. You hear me?" he asked in a low tone.

"Mmmbbbb, huuummmmmbbbb," I said while keeping a mouth full of his penis.

He grabbed the back of my head and began to force it in and out of my mouth. "Yeahhhh, that's it. Damn."

I made the slurping sounds that he loved and I jerked it, from the balls to the tip, just like he'd taught me. "Don't stop, don't stop, Nia."

Two minutes later, his ass cheeks tightened and he squirted gobs of cum into my mouth. "Get all that shit," he said. Some slid out the corners of my mouth but I swallowed most of it.

"Ahhhhhhh," he allowed his head to fall back into the pillow. Three minutes later he was snoring.

Your girl can stay for a little while. I know you been bored," Ali said the next morning. But I ain't supporting no bitch I ain't fucking.

"What's that supposed to mean? You want to fuck her?" I was about to slap the shit out of him.

He laughed, showing his pretty white teeth. "No, that means that after a few weeks, she gotta bounce, or get a job.

"Well if she gets a job, then so will I."

He shrugged his shoulders and shocked the shit out of me. "Well, I guess you two gonna need some I.D. then. I think I can help you with that."

We were in a college town, so finding someone to make fake driver's permits was relatively easy. My reason for the I.D. wasn't really to work. I just thought it would be great if Brandy and I could get into a club from time to time.

Ali came through and a week later, we had social security cards with fake names. I was now Jayla Kennedy and Brandy was Tori Moore.

Not that we were lazy, but neither of us really wanted to work. I had the rest of my life to punch a clock and right now I wasn't mentally prepared to start answering to someone.

First things first, I had to show Brandy the city of Atlanta and we had an absolute blast hanging out at the Underground, Dave & Busters, pretending to be students at Spellman University. We even wore the sweatshirts with the name written across the chest.

For the next couple of weeks I spent most of the money Ali gave me buying clothes for Brandy. She was only a size two and couldn't fit anything that belonged to me. Since she needed everything, I had to scale back on some of the more expensive things, but she was still appreciative.

A few weeks after Brandy arrived, we were on the bus coming back from Lenox Square when Brandy reached down and took my hand. I looked over into her eyes and she stared back. Her skin had returned to the same beauty that I'd always known. Her bruises were gone and she actually looked happy. Out of the blue she said, "Nia, I love you."

"I love you too," I said back. For some reason I thought about Neek. She and I often told one another how lucky and glad we felt to have one another.

"I want to call my mother again, to tell her I'm okay, but I don't think I ever want to go back. I'm happy, maybe for the first time ever. I can't even believe it after all that's happened this year. I still have dreams about the night that Neek was killed, and Shante, even being the snake that she was, we've been friends since the fourth grade. With all of that, I'm still happy." She smiled.

"Well, I'm a lot better since you got here, but to be honest I miss home," I said. "But, not enough to want to go to jail."

She laughed. "Yeah, I feel you. But I don't think it's home you miss. I think it's the people. You mother... DeMarcus."

She'd hit the nail on the head and moved me to silence. We rode without talking for the next few minutes then she said, "I have an idea."

"What?"

"How about if they come down here to visit. DeMarcus and Harold."

"I don't know. I think Harold might run his mouth," I said. "Plus, DeMarcus has a new girlfriend."

"Oh."

"But you can go back and visit whenever you want." I thought about her words for a second then I asked her. "So you like Harold like that?"

"Girllll, hell yeah. Harold is fine as hell and he can work his shit. I know you had to hear me down in the basement that day."

"I actually saw you."

"Noooo," she giggled looking all embarrassed. I imitated her moans and described what I'd seen. I clowned her all the way home.

When we got back to the apartment, Ali was in the kitchen on the phone. He hung up before we could get inside and take a seat. He stormed toward us like he was on a mission and grabbed the bags out of our hands. "Hey," he said.

"What's your problem?" I asked, embarrassed by his behavior.

He wasn't concerned with anything except his own agenda. "All this shit and everything that's in them closets that you haven't worn... all of it is going back to the store. And that car you want me to get you, forget it."

"What?" I asked.

"You heard me. It's all going back."

"Why?"

"Because some shit has gone down and unless you two are ready to do some real work... it's time for cutbacks."

I wasn't sure what he had in mind, but I wasn't planning on taking anything back. "What are you talking about?"

"I'm talking about the fact that I was pulled over by the undercovers today. I had to jump out and leave the van. I had just copped and I had everything in it. Now, I'm broke and I owe my Florida connect a grip. My whole re-up was in the car."

"So what are we gonna do?" I wanted to add, *'to keep from having to take our stuff back.'*

"I got a plan. There's this nigga, Frank Money from Detroit, who comes to town a couple of times a month to do business. He brings a shit load of fishscale and that boy with him when he comes."

"Who's that boy?" Brandy asked in a whisper. Boy was another word for dope. Fishscale was pure compressed cocaine. Though I knew, I didn't want to interrupt Ali, knowing he'd get pissed.

As expected, Ali had ignored her and went on. "While he's in town, he hangs out at this spot called Club Crystal. I got the word from, Big Lenny, one of the bouncers there who I do business with. This cat, Frank, I'm going to rob him."

"That sounds dangerous," I said.

"It won't be. I got the shit all worked out. It's gonna be like taking candy from a baby. He won't know what hit his ass. That's where you two come in. That job you talked about getting... now's the time." We both stood there waiting for more. "You two are going to get a job at Club Crystal."

"Doing what?"

"Dancing."

"Dancing?" Brandy asked.

"Stripping. It's a strip club."

"Oh, Fuck that. I ain't stripping," Brandy said.

"Well you can take your ass back to D.C. And when me and Nia are on the streets and wind up in jail, we'll have you to thank."

"C'mon, Ali. You know we can't be strippers. We only..."

102

"Ya'll got them fake I.D.'s and you both look young, but so does everybody else up in that joint. Put on a little make up and it's all good. Nia, your body is like a grown woman's and Brandy... you sexy too. Just because you're slim don't mean shit." I was a little uncomfortable when he said that. "Look, all you have to do is work for about a week, two at the most. He'll come through and he always goes after the new girls. You play hard to get the first night, the second night he comes back and you go back to his hotel with him. You drug him, call me, and that's it."

"I don't know, that shit seems dangerous," I said.

"Did I say that when you called me to come peel Tony's cap? Listen, this shit is so elementary. Once I get rid of the product, I'll give you both twenty-five grand, to do whatever you want to with it."

"So when you say he goes after the new girls, you mean what? What will he want us to do when he gets us back to the room?"

"He'll probably want you to dance for him. Maybe kiss each other, hell I don't know, but for twenty-five thousand, what the hell."

We were both quiet. Brandy took a seat on the couch and he dropped her bags on the floor next to her. "So are you two down or what?"

Ali was staring directly into my eyes. This man had done everything for me. He fed me, clothed me, and killed for me. Now he was asking me for one thing to *help* him *help* us. "Yeah," I nodded.

Hearing me Brandy chimed in, "Okay, fuck it."

Ali started grinning from ear to ear. "Okay, then. In the morning I'm going to get a rental car and after that, I'm going to take you two to get some tattoos and a couple of outfits. After that we'll go meet, Big Lenny. He's the bouncer I know.

Big Lenny is going to walk you in to the owner and get you hired."

I exhaled and he added, "So think about what types of tats you want. Oh, and as a bonus, you two should make some pretty good money at the club."

"Like how much," Brandy asked as if she was considering dancing for a career move.

"Two, three, hundred…I've heard of girls making a thousand a night. It all depends."

"On what?"

He smiled and said, "Down here, they like when the girls do all kinds of tricks. Clapping their ass cheeks, giving up good lap dances, dropping their asses to the floor, you know… they like it when the girls get low."

Shake that Money Maker
Chapter 11

Brandy and I sat in a booth both in the back of Club Crystal feeling slightly nervous. We were ten minutes from our first time on stage. We were both using the alcohol to chase away our inhibitions. Brandy had nearly freaked out when she realized that we'd have to take our bottoms off as well as our tops. For some reason, that aspect of it wasn't what bothered me. I was proud of my body, I just didn't want any of the perverts touching me. Ali had assured us that the contact was minimal. And the fact that it was only a week made it seem bearable. We'd work four or five days, Frank Money would slide through, we'd do what we had to do and never have to look back according to Ali.

It had been a week since we'd both gotten tatted up. Brandy had gone a little crazy. I had no idea that she'd always wanted to turn her body into a billboard. I personally thought body art was unladylike. Not her though, she'd gotten five of them. Chinese letters saying *'forever beautiful'* on her neck, a serpent on a crucifix on her upper arm, Indian art on her lower back, paw prints on her thigh, and the words 'So Juicy' just below her bikini line.

If I was going to get them, they had to at least have some meaning to me. I decided to get Neek's name inside an Ankh, with butterfly wings attached to it. The Ankh being the Egyptian symbol for life, butterflies signifying rebirth; I designed the tattoo to mean that Neek, gone in the physical, had been reborn. As long as I lived, so would she. One day I would give birth to a child bearing her name, son or daughter.

Dominique would be their name. I think about her everyday and now, I'd take her with me wherever I went in life. I also put the words *so sexy* on the small of my back in the Chinese letters.

For a little extra effect, I'd gotten my belly button pierced. Brandy elected to get holes in her nose and tongue. I'd gotten my first weave and had hair hanging below my shoulders now. Brandy's hair was too fine, so she cut it short. She was sexy, and I was sure she'd attract gay women by the truck load.

The owner of the club was in his late forties and went by the name of Polo. He was pretty cool and went out of his way to make us feel comfortable. He'd bragged to us how he was one of the few owners in the city who hired new girls, gave them a start.

"Ya'll hurrd of Buffy the Body? This is whurr she started. Right thurr on that stage. Sheeeeiiiiittttt," he said in the thick southern accent that seemed to come and go depending on how cool he was trying to be. "Hayuff uh dem bitches you see in dem magazines, done came through hurrr," he said.

We'd spent the first day training on the stage with Destiny, his top dancer. She was the resident trainer. When he told us to show them our moves, all we did was dance as if we were at a go-go back home, only slower. I watched as Polo seemed to become mesmerized. Although it was nothing to be proud of, I had always gotten in trouble for dancing too nasty as a kid, imitating videos on BET, even in elementary school. Brandy did the exact same thing, only she had gotten extra daring and climbed the pole, sliding down into a split. I had mouthed the words, "This bitch is showing off," as I clapped and laughed.

I looked over to see Polo had gone crazy, banging on the table so hard he knocked his beer off the table. "Ya'll two is naturals. Ya'll gonna get paid. You just need to remember to shake dat money maker as much as possible and watch deez niggas spend all they money."

I think his favorite part of the night was when he had us perform lap dances on him to ensure he wouldn't get any complaints. "No, you doing to much," he'd corrected Brandy. "You only getting a dub for this sheeit. Leave em' wanting more and they'll spend it." I went after her and gave a few seductive looks and grinds. "That thurr is perfect," he told me. "Don't look like you're too into it. They'll think you're a freak and try you, gurrl. Act like you doin' deez niggas a favor to only charge em' twenty. And make sure you watch the clock, six or seven minutes, that's it."

I had never realized that there was so much science involved in the world of stripping.

Club Crystal had a reputation throughout the city for having the livest girls. Even though Magic City, The Gold Club and a couple of others were more renowned across the country, every hustler, ball player and politician who liked spending dollars to view flesh made their way to Club Crystal.

On the outside it didn't look like anything special, since it was a renovated Pancake House. But on the inside, top of the line carpet, plush booths, modern furniture and a black, granite bar, made the place look rich. In fact, Polo had rented it out to several rappers, who had used it to shoot videos. A couple of them I'd seen in the club.

At three P.M. we were in the dressing room at our lockers getting ready to perform. Polo had told Brandy to go first. "Tori, I want you to go first. Ice ain't here today and you and her look a little bit alike, so you should do real good. I see a bunch of her customers out there, so go get em."

She and I hugged as she headed out the door. The deejay announced her arrival as if he were giving the vitals for a basketball player stepping onto the court. "Brand new here at Club Crystal, all the way from Baltimore, Maryland, the sweet and sexy, Miss Torrrrrriiiiiiiiii," he yelled as he spun LL Cool J's *Doin It.*

I stood back and watched in amazement as Tori strolled out there as if she was born to do this. The place wasn't packed but the people who were there had taken up all of the seats near the stage so that she was on display, up close and personal. She did the same routine that she'd done in practice only she seemed to be enjoying the attention. Before she even unfastened her top, the men had begun to toss singles onto the stage.

Like a veteran she slowed down and began to play to the men who were tipping. She worked them, giving each man a few moments to stuff some cash into her garter. Then, almost as daring as she'd been that night in my backyard the previous summer, she pulled her bikini top off, exposing her breast. The men started howling when they saw her meaty nipples jutting off her chest.

Her skin was glistening from the oil I'd rubbed on her back and she looked like a stick of caramel. She grinded her hips against an imaginary partner and then did her pole act. She rolled from her split into a position on the stage where she could simulate sex.

As her song changed to *You're Makin' Me High* by Toni Braxton, she slipped off her bottoms. I thought to myself that either she'd done this before or she was drunk. Men walked up to her, and one woman who looked like a teenage boy, one after the other sticking money in her garter. Some of them simply dropped the money onto her belly.

Ones, fives and tens, all in exchange for a brush against her skin. A minute later and the song ended. I snapped out of my trance. It was my turn.

"Can you believe this shit?" I asked.

Ali's connect at the club, Big Lenny, had called a taxi for us and there we were feeling good as hell, in the back of a cab on the way home. Never mind that it was two in the morning. We'd been at the club for nearly twelve hours, but for our trouble Brandy had well over four hundred dollars left after paying Polo two hundred. I had just finished counting seven hundred.

Brandy had laughed it off and said, "Bitch, I knew going in that those big ass titties and that ass of yours was going to be worth at least an extra three hundred dollars."

We were working again tomorrow at five, but we'd get to keep all of our money this time. Polo charged all the dancers' two bills a week to work there, with the cash due on Friday night before you left the club. For this you were guaranteed at least four days of work. I did the math and figured that, even with slow days, we were in a position to make nearly fifteen hundred a week.

As we put our money neatly in stacks and tucked it into our bras we both had smiles on our faces as wide as our ears. I gave the cab driver a twenty on a fourteen dollar ride. "God bless you," he said.

As we walked to the door Brandy grabbed my arm, "Are you thinking what I'm thinking?"

"And that is?"

"Do you know how much money we can make doing this?"

I smiled. "I have an idea."

"So, do you think we should rob that guy and ruin this?"

It was a question worth considering but not doing what we'd already agreed to would mean crossing Ali. I wasn't willing to do that. I was scared to do that. After all, he *was* a killer.

We were off on Wednesday and I asked Ali if I could take him out to say thanks for everything he'd done for me. Beyond the 'thank you' I had something else I wanted to discuss with him. I'd thought long and hard about the risk involved in robbing a big drug dealer and neither Brandy, nor myself, really wanted to do it. I had a plan to use the two things that he loved most to get him to reconsider.

At first he didn't want to miss work to hang out with me, but I begged him and swore that I'd make sure it was worth his while. One of the girls who worked at the club dated a promoter. He was having a show at a club downtown off of Peachtree with Montell Jordan performing and a brand new artist name Erykah Badu opening for him.

Once he agreed to go he went and got a haircut. When he came back home I had a brand new pair of DKNY jeans, a Ralph Lauren sweat shirt and a fresh pair of Timberland boots laid out on the bed for him. On top of that there was a brand new pair of Calvin Klein boxer briefs, an undershirt, socks, and a fresh bottle of Armani cologne.

When he walked out of the bedroom he couldn't stop smiling. "Girl, I don't believe you. You want me fresh from head to toe."

While he showered, I went out into the living room to talk to Brandy. It was easy to convince her to go along with the plan. After only five days she was hooked on staying a dancer,

110

and she wanted to make sure that I was able to stay right by her side.

At the show the chick Erykah Badu ripped it down and had the crowd grooving. She had an album coming out in the fall and after hearing her belt out song after song, I felt as though she had the potential to become a big star. Montell Jordan did well also and when we left the show, Ali was in a really chilled mood. "You want to go get something to eat?" he'd asked.

We'd already had a nice dinner at Ruth's Chris Steak House, so I was good. "Nope, I want to get home. I'm hungry for something else," I said seductively. He nodded and headed toward our spot. We smoked some really strong weed as we drove home. Can you pull over at the QuikTrip and get me some Doritos, a strawberry Fanta, and get Brandy a Slim Jim and…"

"Why don't you just come in?"

"Nah, just grab it for me."

While he was in the store, I called home and told Brandy we were five minutes from the door. It was almost one A.M. and I wanted to make sure she wasn't sleep. "Alright, everything's good," she said.

As we drove the last couple of miles, Ali turned to me and said, "Nia, I want to thank you for tonight. I needed this."

"Baby, you're welcome. You deserve it."

He smiled before continuing. "I know you miss home, but you've been a really good sport. A real trooper. Sometimes, I wish that I didn't get you into all this. Maybe I shouldn't have smashed Tony. I feel like I robbed you."

"Baby, don't second guess yourself." It was strange hearing his thoughts. I knew that everything happened for a reason, even if we didn't understand them. "Tony tried to kill me. He did kill my best friend, my sister. I'm glad he's dead. I just wish you wouldn't have to face any trouble behind it."

"One day, they'll catch me," he said.

"Don't say that."

"It's okay. That's the way it goes. One day, they will. And when that day comes, I'll go like a man. I'll face it." His voice was calm and strong, "But until then, I want to enjoy my life, with you. I love you."

I leaned over and kissed him on the lips as we pulled into our parking lot. When we walked into the apartment the lights were out. The only light came from the flickering candles. There was soft music coming from the bedroom and more candles burning, giving off the scents of green apples, mixed with vanilla.

"What you got goin' on in here?" he asked.

Immediately I began to kiss him and undress him as I led him by his hand to the bedroom. I pulled his shirt off and sat him on the bed. I got down on my knees and loosened up the strings on his left boot and as he wriggled his foot free, Brandy appeared at the door and moved quickly to the other foot. Ali tried to focus his eyes on her as we each yanked off a sock. She was dressed in only a maroon corset and matching thong.

Once his boots were off, we both attacked his belt and had his jeans sliding off in an instant. I moved back up to him and began to kiss him again as I pushed him back onto the bed. Brandy's hands were gripping the sides of his underwear as she removed them, leaving him completely naked.

"What...mmm... Are... you... doing?" he said between my kisses.

"Just relax..." I kissed his neck. "We...got this." I looked down at Brandy and nodded as I gripped his dick. Even while he wasn't hard, several inches spilled beyond my grip. Brandy moved over and I could tell she was shocked at the size even after I'd warned her. Her mouth was small but she did her best to swallow the huge tip along with a few inches.

"Oh, shit," he moaned. I removed my hand and let her go to work as I stood up and undressed in front of him. My breast fell out of my bra and I caressed them, pulling on the nipples. He loved when I did that. I sat on the bed for a second and watched Brandy give my man head. Strangely, I didn't feel one ounce of jealousy.

She was making all kinds of slurping noise as she sucked on his pole, and licked up and down. "Mmmmm," she said now holding his rock-hard cock like a gear shift. I couldn't take any more of what I was seeing.

I climbed on top of his face and smashed my pussy onto his mouth. He responded like the eating machine he was. I gyrated harder than ever as I began to pour my wetness into his mouth. His tongue was a weapon that should have been registered. He was playing a game of tag with my clit while I tried to keep myself from coming to quickly. "Yeahhhh, yesssss, eat it, baby. Suck my pussssyyyy, baby."

I was about to cum when I heard Brandy scream out as if she'd been stabbed. I turned around to see that she had stopped sucking Ali's dick and had impaled herself on it. Like a fool she'd tried to take all ten and half inches. Now she was bucking and shivering like a heroin addict going through the shakes. The dick was about to short circuit her brain. I'd been there.

I continued riding his face as I leaned back enough to watch her drifting between pain and pleasure. As I saw signs in her face that the pain had begun to give way to ecstasy, I lost control and enjoyed my first orgasm.

I climbed up off of him and he wiped his mouth, which was coated with my juices. Immediately, Ali grabbed Brandy's hips and started to give her the type of fucking that a john gave a whore. He bounced her one hundred pound frame up and down on him until she screamed like a baby. "Oooohhhhhhwwwwwweeeeeeeeee," she cried out. "Ohhhhhh shit. This dick is so ... fucking... big."

I started to caress her breast and even sucked her nipples. The sight of me touching her sent Ali over the top and he yelled out, "Fukkkkk, I'm about to nut."

"Meee toooooo," Brandy moaned out as they both came at the same time, him shooting his seed deep into her womb and her spilling her juices all over his manhood.

Now I was jealous.

Brandy and I took turns fucking him for the next hour and a half until he begged us to let him rest. He woke up at four-thirty in the morning with one of us on each side of him.

"Did I die and go to heaven?" he asked as he stood up to go piss. When he came back to bed I was sitting up.

"Baby, I want to talk to you about something," I said.

"If it's about the way I fucked her, there is no way I would ever do that again without you saying…"

"No it's not that. As a matter of fact, I hope you enjoyed that."

"How could I not have?"

"Well that's good, because both Brandy and I want you to be able to keep enjoying it."

"Really?" He sat down on the edge of the bed and began to stroke my leg.

"Yeah. But the thing is this… we been thinking about it and we both… we don't feel good about robbery thing. We want to be able to keep on dancing. If we keep dancing, we'll have money to chip in and then you can take your time getting back on your feet, plus…"

He took a deep breath before cutting me off. "Let me say this to you one time. You two are going to do this thing for me and that's all there is to it. I owe motherfuckers money. This shit ain't no joke. These, Jacksonville boys will come up here and kill me and you and then go to D.C. and kill your mama, my grandmamma and they cats and dogs. Plus the time is now for me to take over. I don't have no time to start from the ground up. You want me on the corner serving the fucking police? Is that what you want?" His voice was angry and I knew then that I had no choice.

"No... I don't..."

"Then don't bring this shit up again. Frank should be in town within the next week or so. We gonna do this," he laughed. He stood up and headed for the bathroom. "Is that why you took me out?"

"No, I wanted to show you that..."

"Shut the fuck up and wake Brandy's skinny ass up and tell her to go get on the fucking couch. Ya'll bitches must be crazy."

He slammed the door to the bathroom and turned the shower on. Brandy looked up at me and saw the look on my face.

"It's okay," she said. "It's gonna be okay."

Cutting to the Chase
Chapter 12

Two more weeks blew by before Frank Money finally showed up at the club. By that time, Brandy and I were becoming the talk of the ATL strip scene. The liquor licensing board had even popped through Club Crystal and checked everyone's I.D.s. Our's passed with flying colors and everything was good for Polo. We had people coming back day in and day out and with the drink minimum, Polo was cleaning up.

He kept calling us his Baltimore connection. Of course that's where Ali had told us to tell him we were from. "My Baltimore girls are haaawwwwt," he'd brag to every person who came through the door. By the end of the third week, we were starting to encounter a little bit of jealousy from a couple of the other girls.

Destiny had warned us ahead of time. When Brandy got upset a comment one of the girls had made, calling her a skinny bitch. "Don't worry bout' dat shit. It'll take care of itself. Jealousy eats people up from inside out. Most times, if you ignore a jealous bitch, you hurt her twice as bad. Just don't give it any energy. Focus on making that money while you can, cause' next week, next month, or next year, it'll be some more new bitches. Big ol' booties and maybe even pretty like your Indian-princess-looking ass," she said in a playful manner. "Fuck deze lazy ho's. Get dat paper, by any means necessary."

And get paper we did. The third week I'd made two thousand dollars to Brandy's sixteen hundred. Getting the men to part ways with their hard earned money was too easy.

The first night when Frank Money came into the club, he didn't look like anything special. The pair of sweatpants and a button-down collar shirt he wore had me wondering if this was the right man. This guy was slim and small, not even five foot six. He wore a close cut with a part down the middle of it and had one gold-plated tooth that he showed when he smiled, which seemed to be every few minutes. The picture that I was seeing didn't fit with what I'd imagined for a big-time dealer.

Big Lenny walked past me and gave me the nod to be sure I knew for certain who he was. It was a Thursday night and if it hadn't been for Frank Money, it would have been slow. All the girls loved when he came through. He was good to toss three or four thousand around the club without blinking, and he'd done exactly that.

He definitely seemed to take a liking to Brandy, asking her to have a drink with him at his table. She sat down and made small talk with him. While I was dancing, Brandy waved me over to them. I smiled and when I finished my set, I went over and greeted them. "This is Jayla. Jayla, Frank Money."

"Nice to meet you," I said as I gave him a grin and a handshake. When she stated that she was going to be riding home with her new friend I said, "Excuse us for a moment."

We walked away from the table as the plan called for, and I asked how it was going.

"He's a horny motherfucker, so you know how it's going," she laughed. "But he's actually kind of a smooth talker. He reminds me of a pimp from one of them old movies we used to watch."

"Well, now you gotta go break the news to him. I'll go to the bar and wait for you to come looking for me."

Brandy went over and told him that I'd reminded her of our rules. *One didn't leave without the other when dealing*

117

with strangers. Of course he asked that I come over and as soon as I reached the table he started talking about how much money he'd pay us to go back to his spot with him.

"Mr. Money," I said.

"Call me Frank or Money. Or you can call me Frank Money, but not Mister Money."

"Okay, Frank. I'm sorry about this but tonight is bad for us. We work tomorrow and will be better prepared for you, if you're still interested. I think your offer was very generous, but Tori, here seems to have forgotten a prior obligation."

"An obligation that can't be broken for three grand?"

"Sorry, but no it can't." I looked down at the table at his cognac and coke. "What are you drinking?"

"Remy and Coke, sweetheart. Why you wanna drink?"

"No, but a friend of mine works at a liquor store out in Buckhead. He gets some of the best stuff for cheap. If you wanna take us up on our offer for tomorrow, I can bring you a bottle of Louis XIII. You ever had that?"

"Baby, what you know about that," he said as he bobbed his head. "That's a sixteen hundred dollar bottle of liquor."

"Yeah, well I can get a bottle for about three hundred."

"Okay, well I'll tell you what. Bring two and you have a deal. I'll pay you five hundred each."

"Well, the one bottle is a gift, but if you'd like a second, I'll see what I can do."

"Okay, sweetheart. I'll see you ladies tomorrow."

As we prepared to make our escape, Big Lenny sent another girl over to keep him occupied while we grabbed our things and headed out the door.

The next night, Frank Money took us into a quiet neighborhood in an upscale single-family development out in Stone Mountain instead of a hotel as we'd expected. The entire time, I sat nervously in the back seat of the Mercedes he drove, all the while wanting to look back to make sure that Ali had been able to follow us.

When we pulled up to the house the garage door lifted up and we entered. Once we piled out of the car and walked into the house I began to wonder when Ali's plan would kick in. How long would it take before he came bursting through the door.

Instead Frank turned on some music and told us to make ourselves comfortable. "I've got one piece of business to attend to and then we can get down to business ladies. So excuse me for a few minutes."

Brandy shrugged her shoulders, took a seat, and began sifting through a stack of CD's on the glass coffee table. We were in the basement sitting on a thick-cushioned, S-shaped couch that stretched across two thirds of the wall. There was a plasma television mounted over a fireplace, a few free-standing video games, including my favorite, Ms. Pac-Man, and a pinball machine. The place had the feel of a true bachelor pad. I imagined leopard print sheets and leather upstairs, but didn't really want to see any more.

"He don't have shit. All this music is from the eighties. Bobby Brown, The Time, Patti Labelle, Rick James... and who the fuck is Bobby Womack?" she said.

"Don't ask me," I said as I pulled my phone out of my purse. I dialed Ali's number. It began to ring, but I didn't get an answer. Instead of putting it back in my bag I stuffed it into the pocket of my jeans.

I heard the doorbell ring and instantly my heart began to beat fast. As I envisioned Ali coming through the door guns blasting, I had a flashback of the night when I witnessed the shoot out between Ali's friend, Kurt, and the police. I couldn't help but wonder if gunfire was about to break out.

Instead a few seconds later Frank came back down the steps followed by three other men. "Ladies, here are a couple of my partnas. I told them that we were about to have a little fun, and they wanted to join in so... the more the merrier, right?"

Brandy looked at me with a stunned look. Then she said, "You said we were dancing for you. The price we gave you was for you."

"No problem, beautiful," one of the men said as he walked up to her and gave her a forceful hug. "Cleve, break em' off something extra."

Cleve, who looked like Mr. T., minus the Mohawk haircut, tossed me a wad of cash rolled up in a rubber band.

"Don't be cheap," Frank added, "These is the finest bitches in the fucking club."

"Cleve, toss em' two more, what the fuck I care," Mike said.

Cleve said, "Mike, that was a G."

"Nigga, I said toss them two more."

He hesitated and the fourth man, who'd been quiet walked over to where I was seated and handed me a stack of money. "How are you. My name is Jermaine. This is my home."

Jermaine was tall and handsome, and he didn't seem to fit in with the other three. He offered me his hand and I shook it. "Hey, I'm Jayla and that's Tori."

"Ya'll not from the ATL are you?"

"No, we from up north."

"Okay, well can I get you anything? Some food or drinks."

"No we're okay. Actually, I brought something for Frank. It's in my bag." I pulled out the liquor that Ali had given me to give them. He'd instructed me to make a drink for

Frank and if I got the chance to slip a couple of tabs of Ecstasy into his drink. He'd be dazed and easy to control. It might keep him from having to get killed. This was before the other men showed up and now I didn't know how this was going to unfold.

A minute later Frank had Bobby Brown, blasting through the speakers. *'Girllll, as long as I been giving my love to you... yoooouuuu should be giving meeee your love tooooo..."*

"Let's get this party started," Mike yelled out.

Jermaine said, "Go ahead and put your money away. Are you going to change?"

"Uhhhhmmm, yeah. I also need to use the bathroom."

"Follow me. Your girl can start." I looked over at Brandy and saw that Cleve and Frank were passing some weed with her."

Jermaine led me upstairs and pointed to a room in the back. "The second door, on the left."

I walked into the bathroom and closed the door. The marble floors were nice and the copper-colored wall paper gave it a rich look. I took my phone out and ran the water. I started calling Ali, back to back. Still no answer. I was getting pissed and was ready to slam the phone against the wall.

I needed to get a grip before I lost it. Needed to think. *Maybe they knew it was a set up and were going to kill us. Maybe Ali had gotten lost and was riding around the neighborhood.* I called back and when his machine came on, I tried to recall as much as I could. "Ali, I don't remember the house number, but it's a brick house. Frank pulled his car into the garage, but some other guys pulled up. There was... I think there's a fountain in the middle of the front yard. Hurry up," I whispered.

I took my time and called back four more times with each detail I remembered. I recalled the fact that there was no side walk in front of the house, the dark color of the garage door that it had small windows on it. Finally, there was a knock at the door.

"You alright," Jermaine asked.

"Here I come," I said. In a flash, I pulled my pants off and switched into a bikini. I was going to have to dance for these guys or risk them getting suspicious, angry or both. Though I hadn't been paying full attention, I realized at that point that we'd collected almost five thousand dollars from Frank, Cleve and Jermaine. Even still, my heart was beating so fast that I feared I might pass out. Out of desperation I reached into my pocket and pulled out one of the pills Ali had given me for Frank. I tossed one into my mouth and washed it down with water from the sink.

After packing my stuff into my bag, I opened the door. Jermaine greeted me in the hallway with, "Damn, girl. Wow. I didn't know it was like that." A fake smile sprung forth. I was nervous. He went on. "Hey, listen," Your girl is down there dancing and Frank said that he really only wanted her. He has a thing for petite women. I figured that maybe you could dance for me, up here." He reached into his pocket. "Here's another five hundred."

"I guess." At this point I was so pissed at Ali that I couldn't think straight.

The music downstairs was blasting so loud that the floor was vibrating. He led me into the back room. Inside of his room, there was black carpet on the floor, a circle shaped bed and a one hundred and fifty-gallon fish tank built into the wall. This man had made a small fortune selling drugs, I assumed.

He sat down on the edge of the bed and hit the remote. When D'Angelo started playing, I closed my eyes. I gyrated slowly, spun around for him and dropped to the floor. I began to lose track of time as I gave him a lap dance. The ecstasy was beginning to take over my mind. One track after the other played completely through, but it felt as if only a few seconds had passed.

I didn't mind that Jermaine's hands were all over my body. In fact, they began to feel good. My skin was tingling and every time he touched me, it sent chills through my body. Out of the blue I pulled my top off, grabbed my breasts and pushed them together. "I want you... to lick both of my nipples at the same time."

"Yeah, okay," he laughed. "You kinda wild, huh?"

"Do you like me?" I asked. "I like you. Do you like me?"

"Yeah, I like you," he responded as he tried to concentrate on my tits.

My nipples were more sensitive than ever and I started to rub violently on my pussy. "Oh, shit," I moaned and sucked my own tongue. "Ssssslllllllll....uuuuhhhhmmmm," I was making all types of weird noises.

I didn't put up a fight or a fuss. I was now officially rolling off of the E. I don't remember him pulling off my bikini because he didn't. Instead he merely pulled the material covering my crotch to the side. Once he'd slipped on the rubber, I felt him pushing his dick inside of me. He was doing his best to jackhammer me as he had me on his bed on all fours, but he wasn't packing enough to do any damage. After getting fucked by Ali for all these months, his four-inch dick was only teasing me.

Still, my body was so wound up of off the drugs that any amount of dick felt good. I didn't want Jermaine to stop. But he did. He grunted and came hard. I started laughing and sat down on the bed for a second. While he panted, I stood up and headed for the door to use the bathroom. I thought about

Brandy and decided to go check on her, so titties exposed and bouncing, I walked down the hallway and headed for the steps.

The music was still blasting. When I reached the basement, I didn't see anyone and began to worry. I walked around the corner and saw a door that I hadn't noticed earlier. I moved to it and turned the knob. When I opened it, there was Brandy being held down by Cleve and Mike while Frank Money fucked her in the ass yelling out, "Yeah, that's it. Hold the bitch still."

Brandy was screaming at the top of her lungs. I panicked and ran back up the steps into the kitchen, knocking over microwave stand as I searched the drawers for a knife. I scrambled through three of them before I found a butcher knife that I felt would do the job. When I noticed a two-pronged, grilling fork in the sink, I grabbed that too. I started back out of the kitchen and Jermaine saw me moving frantically. "What's going on?" he asked while walking up the hall but naked.

"They are raping her," I yelled as I raced down the steps, a bikini-clad, killing machine, armed with a deadly instrument in both hands.

"What?" he yelled out and raced after me.

He was too slow to prevent my next move. By the time he caught up to me, I had burst into the room and plunged the fork deep into Frank's back. I yanked it out and plunged it in a second time. He howled like a werewolf as he fell off the side of the bed to the floor. Cleve and Mike both jumped back, "Bitch, what are you doing?"

"Ya'll motherfuckers gonna die," I said as I charged Mike. He put his hands out in front of his face and the knife punched through his palm as if it was made of tissue paper.

"Ahhhhhhhhh," Mike's scream was louder than Frank's. Brandy recoiled as she saw the blood pouring out of Mike's palm as he'd fallen onto the bed next to her.   She jumped up, eyes wide open, still in shock, as I swung the knife and fork trying my best to take an eye out of Mike's head. Cleve was in the corner cowering like a bitch, trying to avoid the attack. All of them were naked and vulnerable. They'd gone from waiting their turn for Brandy to hoping that they wouldn't get a turn to feel my wrath.

It didn't work out well for them, as my next attempt with the fork hit Mike's shoulder so hard, his bone bent the tip of the fork. He passed out when a stream of blood shoot out of his body like a water fountain. This time he fell off the mattress and slid to the ground. "Grab that bitch, Jermaine. I'm going to kill her," Frank said weakly. He was loosing blood and had the look of a punch-drunk fighter.

Jermaine was smart enough to stay back.

At the top of my lungs I barked out, "Get your shit, girl. And then go upstairs and get my bag from out of the back room." I grabbed the fork from the floor next to Mike. "Move your ass over there Jermaine or I will cut your dick off and feed it to you."

He moved over to the other side of the bed. Then Cleve said, "We gotta get Frank to a hospital." He should have been worried about Mike who seemed to be in worse shape.

"Fuck Frank," I yelled. "He raped my girl. He can die in this motherfucker."

"He didn't rape her, he paid her extra to fuck her in the ass."

"Shut the fuck up or I promise I'll cut your tongue out your ugly ass face."

Brandy came back and I said, "Look in the pocket on the bottom of the bag. Is the money still in there?"

"Yeah," she said.

"Where the fuck are your keys, Jermaine?"

"By the front door," he said sounding scared. "On the steps."

"Tori, go grab the keys and start the car, get in the passenger's seat and hit the horn.

She took off and followed the directions.

Sixty seconds later, I ran out into the cold night air in nothing but a bikini bottom and jumped into Jermaine's Lexus GS300.

We pulled out of the driveway and sped out of the neighborhood doing sixty it seemed. I didn't slow down to a speed limit until we reached the highway headed toward the city.

Brandy cried as she confessed to me that she had only agreed to jerk Frank Money off because he'd offered her more money. Then out of nowhere, Cleve had smacked her, choked her, and dragged her to the room. Mike had threatened to kill us both and throw our bodies in the woods. I promised her that we were finished with the dancing. As I drove perfectly across Abernathy Freeway, I apologized over and over for getting her involved.

Strange as it might have been, I felt like laughing when she described how I'd come in there like Norman Bates. "I ain't never seen no shit like that, Nia."

But still, I took a deep breath every few seconds and the entire ride home. She kept saying, "You might have killed those dudes. How the hell can you be so calm?"

"I don't know. I did take one of those pills."

"You're high?"

"Definitely."

With the ecstasy still in my system, I was higher than I'd ever been off of weed. When we got back home a little after three in the morning, I couldn't go to sleep. I sat watching television with Brandy huddled next to me. With each passing moment, my desire for more violence shifted closer to home. I wanted to kill Ali because he'd left us to fend for ourselves.

At eight o'clock the next morning, the television was still on. Brandy had shaken me to consciousness. I looked at the screen and there was footage on the morning news from the night before. A man in his twenties had been taken into custody. Officers had attempted to pull the man over for running a red light in Stone Mountain. After the man fled, a chase ensued, lasting twenty minutes and ended with the suspect crashing into a guard rail and flipping the car over. The suspect was able to climb out of the vehicle himself but was quickly subdued. Searching the vehicle, the police found several assault weapons in the man's car and took the man into custody.

The man was Ali.

In Security

Chapter 13

I didn't know what to do once Ali was locked up. I never realized how much he'd done my thinking for me until he was no longer there. After I'd gone ballistic the night of our caper, stabbing Frank and his boy, I was afraid to show up for work. The first few days, I called out sick, and sat in the apartment trying to come up with a plan. With no one to bounce an idea off of, I felt completely alone.

I didn't blame Brandy, who was understandably off, for the lack of input or conversation. Initially, I couldn't tell if she was angry with me or if she was merely traumatized by what had happened to her. The only thing that I was able to get out of her was that she agreed we shouldn't go back to Club Crystal. In the days following all she did was stay glued to the television.

For the most part, she acted as if the rape hadn't affected her, but all of a sudden, she had an insatiable desire to stay high and drink twenty-four hours a day. She never brought up what happened that night, and I didn't want her to get tired of me asking, *'You okay?'* every ten minutes. So, I did what I thought was best and kept plenty of weed and liquor in the apartment to accommodate her.

Ali's arrest had turned me upside down. I spent days on end thinking of my next move, wondering if my time was coming as well. I wound up buying some over the counter sleeping pills after Brandy had commented on how tired I looked. With my body needing rest, the Unisom kicked in with a fury. The

128

first night I took them, I was on the couch drooling after having dozed off. It was after three in the morning and a bang came at the door. My heart almost leapt out of my chest as I sat up. I looked around for Brandy, but she had already gotten in the bed.

The knocks came again amplified by the quiet of the night. My survival instincts kicked in and I stood up and tiptoed past the door to the kitchen and grabbed a knife. As I approached the door, I heard a deep voice, a real Barry White-sounding, nigga on the other side say, "Jayla, it's Big Lenny from the club."

I thought for a moment about whether or not it was safe to open the door. If he was coming to do me harm, he would be able to crush me like a grape. My mind then went to the fact that Ali had trusted Big Lenny and I couldn't think of any reason he'd want to hurt us. I ran and grabbed some sweats and hid the knife behind the pillow cushion just in case.

"Here I come." I opened the door and flicked on the lights. As usual Big Lenny had on a pair of black cargo pants, military style boots and a tight fitting T-shirt with 'security' across the chest. "What's up?"

"I was coming to check on you two. I went to see Ali and he has some things that he wants you to do."

"How did you know where we lived?" I asked suspiciously.

"Ali, how else?"

"Oh, yeah." I offered him a seat once I'd taken the one next to my knife.

According to Big Lenny, Ali felt it would be a bad idea for me to come to visit him. Instead, he asked me to come up with a thirty-five hundred dollar retainer for a lawyer, who would let him pay the balance of his fees in installments. He didn't want me facing a chance of getting locked up during a visit, even though at this point, he hadn't been linked to the crime back home.

Then he said, "I heard about what happened that night when you went with Frank Money."

"How?"

"One of my boys works for the guy Jermaine, the one whose house you went to for the private show. Jermaine told him about what went down and I'm hearing that he got really upset with the way Frank Money conducted himself with Tori, especially since they were in his house. What made it worse was that this wasn't the first time Frank has gotten out of line, but the word on the street is that this shit was the last straw. From what I hear, Frank is no longer with us."

"What?"

"Don't be surprised. The guy, Jermaine, he's cousins with the Randall brothers."

"The *who* brothers?"

"The Randall brothers, them niggas run damn near half of the Atlanta drug scene. If Jermaine wants somebody finished, then it's automatic."

"Did you hear that he was upset with us?"

"Actually, the opposite. My man said that he wants to get in touch with you, which explains why I've seen him in the club a couple times this week."

"What if he's coming to take us out?" Big Lenny started laughing. "What the hell is so funny? You just said that he's prone to taking motherfuckers out."

"Nah, it's just that you're way off. For some reason I get the feeling that he must be into you. If he wanted you dead, you would have been bodied the next day. Seriously, you don't have to worry about that."

Switching the subject back to Ali I asked, "So what do I need to do about the money?"

"You need to come back to work and make it unless you sitting on something I don't know about. That is, if you want to help Ali."

"Of course I want to help. Can you come and get me tomorrow? There are a few errands I need to run. And also, how do I get the money to this lawyer?"

"Here you go." He placed a card on the table. "What time do you need me?"

"By twelve. I need to go and get a new cell phone and pick up a few things from the store. Most important though, I want you to get me in touch with the guy Jermaine. I need to know this whole thing is squashed before I go back to the club. I don't want to be a sitting duck. And Brandy... I mean Tori, probably won't be ready for a while."

He nodded his head and smiled. "Don't trip, Ali has always called you two by your real names. And as far as Jermaine, I got your back. From what I hear, he's a good dude. I'm on it."

"Do you know if he ever found his car?"

"Yeah, you left it outside of Neiman Marcus double parked with the hazards on?" he asked and laughed again. "He has a personal salesperson there. Once security found the car, she wound up going to pick him up."

The next day I had lunch with Jermaine Randall at the Atlanta Grill on Peachtree Street. My mission was simple. Since he was apparently, a big time drug dealer, I wanted to know if I needed to find another town to lay my head in. We took our seats and he kept smiling at me, nervously almost.

As soon as the waiter had taken our orders, I cut to the chase. "Is it true you fell out with Frank over what he did to my friend?"

"I see people are talking." He laughed and took a sip of his water. "I'll just say it was something like that."

"Maybe you can answer my next question a little more clearly. Is it true that I don't have to worry about *him* coming to the club trying to get some type of revenge for me stabbing his ass?"

"There is no way you'll see him at your club, or *any* club," he laughed. "Frank Money had been messing up for quite some time. My cousins and myself... we're men of principal. We don't believe in doing crud ball shit like that. He was finished in the ATL a while ago, but he kept pushing his luck."

"What about the other two?"

"Cleve and Mike... they're harmless. You saw how they acted when you went Jason Vorhees on they punk asses. Plus, without Frank to look after them, they tucked their tails and went on back to Detroit."

"And you and I..."

"I owe you and your friend an apology. I figured I'd start with this." He handed a set of keys across the table. "That was nice of you to return it but, I don't keep cars too long anyway." It was the keys to his Lexus.

"Are you serious?"

"On one condition." Here it was he was about to crack for some more pussy. I was shocked when he said, "That condition is that we simply, remain friends."

"*Friends*?"

"Yeah. I don't know what it is about you, but I want to remain your *friend*."

"Anything to do with my phat ol' ass?" I asked with a laugh.

He laughed too. "Well that's real nice, but no. Jayla, I like your spirit. I like the way you defended your homegirl

132

even though you didn't know what was going to happen. On top of that you face your problems head on like a soldier. You came here to meet me not knowing what was going down." He sipped his water, took a cube of ice in his mouth and added, "You're loyal and you got heart, and I always need loyal people around me."

"So that's it. Stay your friend, for a Lexus?"

"Showty, you just don't know about me. I could have just as easily given you a bouquet of flowers. A car don't mean much to me. I buy a new one every other month. But stick close and you'll see."

The lunch had me feeling much better about everything. I didn't have any real attraction to Jermaine, except for the fact that he was nice and obviously paid. Beyond that, he seemed like a good person to have on your side.

I left with a few more questions answered about how I'd go on. Like Ali, Jermaine had connections at the DMV and could get the car registered. When he told me that he had people who could get tags, I thought about my BMW and wondered if he could help me get it back on the road, that way Brandy would have a car to drive too.

I took his cell number and promised to call him when I picked up a new one. He dropped me off at the Lexus, which he was having detailed at a shop out in Roswell, and I headed home. I called Big Lenny, thanked him and let him know I'd be back at work. Although my motivation now was strictly for money, deep inside I had sort of missed being on the stage watching men drool and toss their hard earned money for pussy that they'd never get.

It took the authorities another week and a half to discover that Ali had been using an alias, Douglass Mason the whole time he'd been sitting in the Dekalb County Jail. He might have gotten away with it if someone hadn't noticed that the same Douglass Mason whose identity had been stolen, was seventy six years-old and white.

Things went downhill for Ali quickly after that. The lawyer ate the first piece of the retainer like a Scooby snack and did absolutely nothing to stop his extradition back to D.C. His man Kurt had recently been convicted of first degree murder, and now was agreeing to testify against Ali in exchange for leniency.

I was at work when Big Lenny pulled me to the side, "Ali's being shipped back tomorrow morning."

I'd just finished my first set and the news hit me hard. I couldn't believe that his life would never be the same. With what he was about to get convicted of, there was almost no chance that he'd ever walk the streets again. I sat in the dressing room in the corner and began to cry.

I had my head down as the tears poured out while I tried to have a moment of unnoticed grief. *This is all my fault. I did this to Ali.*

"Hey, girl, you okay?" I looked up to see Destiny. Seeing my tears she sat down. "What's wrong?"

Destiny had been as close to a mentor as I could have had since I'd started at Club Crystal. "I'm fine. I just have a lot on my mind."

She said the magic words, "It might help if you talk about it. I'm on break. I'll clear your set and you can come with me. We'll go grab some a bite and you can share whatever you're willing." I wiped my eyes. She added, "Baby, we all need someone to talk to."

Destiny had no idea how much I needed someone. I took her up on her offer and we drove to the Waffle House at the next exit. Even though it was nearly empty we still grabbed a seat in the far rear section. For the next thirty minutes I shared as much as I could about my life, without letting her know my possible involvement in any crime. I didn't put it past anyone turning me in for a few thousand dollars, assuming there was a reward.

"You can't blame yourself. Men do what they do, not for you, but for themselves. Somewhere in all this, your man acted for his own gain. Pride, money, pussy, and power; those are the only things men go to war and kill over. The fact that he brought you down here and has you stripping in a club, under-aged at that, should tell you something."

My mouth dropped open. "I'm eighteen," I said.

"Whatever," she said, "Where do you think you got the fake I.D.'s from?"

"You?"

"A bitch has to have a side hustle. That's why Polo and I are so tight. I help him out with things like that. But don't trip. You ain't the first and you won't be the last sixteen-year old to shake yo' ass in a strip club.

Like I said, your man is going to be fine. He's damn near thirty, he knew what he was doing."

"No, Ali was twenty."

She laughed in my faced. "Are you serious? Did you really think that?"

"He told me…" she cut me off.

"Let me tell you one thing that you should never forget. Believe nothin' you hear and only half of what you see. I guess you didn't read the paper last week. The write-up they had on him… your boy was twenty-eight."

Lying sonofabitch. I needed to see that for myself to be sure, but it made sense. Destiny and I sat and talked for another hour. She made me feel better as she told me that I could really get used to the whole stripping thing as a way to get ahead. "Go to hair school, open a business. By the time you're twenty-five you'll be set," she promised. "Just don't get caught in the booty shake trap. Don't get addicted to the money, because fast money is just that, fast to come and fast to go. You have to build something for yourself. I'm twenty-six and I will be finished with this in four years."

"What are you going to do when you finish?"

"I'm going to see the world. Shop in Paris, Tokyo and Italy."

"You're saving your money to travel?"

"No, I'm going to become a flight attendant."

"Wow, that sounds interesting." I tried to imagine her moving up and down the aisle of a plane with her bodacious ass.

"Yeah, but the reason I'm saving my money is so that I can purchase a Laundromat out in Sandy Springs, and with the money it brings in, I'll be able to do what I enjoy, which is traveling, and still be well off. My uncle owns the Laundromat now, but he's retiring in four years and we've already signed the paperwork. I'm paying him piece by piece."

"That's incredible."

"Not really. Everybody has to have a dream, and most importantly, a plan, big or small. Something to hold on to when life throws you them fucking curveballs."

I nodded in agreement.

We left and went back to work. The club was slow so I prepared to take off early and headed home.

When I was almost home, I clicked on V103, still feeling sad, but trying to pull it together. The group Jade was singing their hit from a couple years earlier. *Five, four, three, two, Yo time is up. Five, four, three, two, Yo time is up. Five, four, three, two, Yo time is up.*

I thought about Ali and thought about the words. I was sixteen years old, on my own in Atlanta. I had my whole life ahead of me. His time was up.

I walked up the steps to my building and turned the key. When I walked through the door of my apartment and saw *him* standing there, at the door I couldn't believe it.

"Surprise," he said.

My eyes told DeMarcus that he was indeed right. This was a surprise.

Friends
Chapter 14

I now realized what people meant when they said that the best surprise *is* no surprise. Seeing DeMarcus in the living room sent a rush of emotions through me that almost caused me to have a panic attack. I loved him, but I didn't even pretend to have the courage to let go and be loved back. Seeing him up close and personal, knocked down the wall I'd put up around myself, exposing me to all my fears and insecurities. Made the feelings real for me again.

Brandy had to have filled them in on the details of our life and I was instantly ashamed that he had to know that I was stripping for a living. Last and most important, a huge part of me didn't trust him, or anyone, with knowing my whereabouts, the information that could cause me to lose my freedom.

Brandy was on the couch hugged up with Harold. For the first time in at least a month, she actually looked happy. Wondering if I'd ever see her in the arms of a man again after what she'd been through, I had to admit that I was slightly relieved. Harold yelled, "What's up, cousin?"

"Hey," I said in a half-hearted tone. Then I locked eyes with DeMarcus. "What are you doing here?" I asked with a half smile.

"What do you mean?" he responded. "I came all this way to see you. Brandy told me that you weren't seeing Ali any more." He wrapped his arms around me and held me tight.

I looked over at Brandy and she said, "He begged me to keep it a surprise, Nia. I told him that you were working a lot lately, but he still wanted to come."

DeMarcus chimed in, "So you're doing telemarketing, huh?"

"Say what?"

"Brandy said that you're working for a telemarketing company now downtown. That's good."

"Oh,…uhh… y… yeah…" I stuttered out. "It's…not much, but just… uhhm, ya' know paying some bills."

"So are you tired, or do you want to go get something to eat?"

"I am tired," I said, then said, "Brandy, I need you to come here for a second. Ya'll excuse me for a second." I pulled her into the room and shut the door. "What the fuck, girl? Why would you do some shit like this?"

Brandy snapped back in a sharp tone, "Listen, Nia, I'm not trying to hear all that. You would have said 'no' if I'd asked. So I didn't bother. Your cousin is not going to rat you out and DeMarcus is in love with you in case you haven't noticed.

Ali's ass is gone, you have no reason to front on your man. They're only staying a couple of days. So just enjoy it. It ain't like you don't need some dick," she laughed.

It was strange hearing her break it down for me as if she wasn't the same bitch who'd been moving around as if she were a foot away from being comatose.

"Brandy, you still can't go around making decisions for me about who I have to trust with *what* information. If I get caught, you don't have to go to jail with me. So I'd appreciate if you don't do any shit like this again."

"Yeah, okay," she said, brushing off my words. I thought for a split second about slapping the shit out of her, but the urge quickly passed.

I hopped in the shower after I put my bag containing my stripper gear into the back of the closet. The hot water was relaxing after the stressful day I'd had so I stood under the water for nearly twenty minutes. By the time I got out Brandy had lit up some of the Purple Haze I'd gotten for her. There was a half-empty bottle of Hypnotiq on the table, sitting next to a bottle of Hennessy. All three of them were drinking Incredible Hulks as they passed the blunt.

"There she is," DeMarcus slurred out. "You look so beautiful." He was high as hell already.

I had a towel on my head, a tank top and a pair of boxers. I laughed at him. "So, how did you all get down here?"

Harold and DeMarcus smiled at each other. "My pops copped me a ride for my birthday last weekend," Harold bragged.

"Oh yeah. What kind?"

"Dodge Intrepid. Black on black."

"Nice. So you put it right on the road?"

"To come and see my two favorite girls, for sho'," he shot back.

"Off the no-bullshit, Harold. You didn't tell your peeps where you were coming, did you?"

"You know they don't pay attention to me any more. I could have flown my ass to Africa and they wouldn't notice. And of course I wouldn't tell them."

"Because, you know they'll tell my mother and she'll think she's doing what's right and fuck around and have me brought back home…"

He cut me off. "Nia, cut that shit out. We family. I know the game and the last thing I want is for you to get in trouble."

He passed the blunt to Brandy. Then out of nowhere DeMarcus chimed in, "Plus, you don't have to worry about that shit no more."

Harold shook his head 'no' trying to keep him from saying something. "Why you say that?"

The two locked into a stare, "Fuck that," DeMarcus said to Harold. "We all in, nigga."

"What are you talking about?" I asked.

DeMarcus pulled me down into the chair he was in and started to rub my shoulders as he spoke. "We found out that your girl, Shante, was being home schooled for the past couple of months."

I finally took a pull of the weed, "Yeah, and?"

"Well, I watched how they were working for a while. Seeing what time the tutor would come and leave."

"For what?"

Ignoring my question he went on. "A couple of weeks ago, the tutor left, I knocked on the door. She let me in. I was going to shoot her, but I lost my nerve."

"What," I said almost gasping.

He went on, "I punched the bitch as hard as I could."

My mouth dropped open. "Knocked her ass out cold as shit. Then I put a bag over her head until she stopped breathing."

I looked over at Brandy who was nodding as if she was listening to her favorite song on the radio instead of a murder confession. "You killed her?" I asked.

"Now you can come home," Harold said. "She was the only person who could tie you what happened.

"All you have do is say that Ali forced you to come down here against your will, that's if you even get charged with anything," DeMarcus added. "You have an alibi. You were at work when it went down."

"How do you know?"

They looked at Brandy. I grabbed the bottle of Hennessy and put it to my mouth. Chugged it like a bottle of Hawaiian

Punch as it burned my throat. Either I couldn't comprehend, or couldn't believe, what they were saying.

The room began to spin. I stood and tried to make it to the bathroom. I reached the toilet and attempted to vomit. Instead all I could do was cry. *What had my life become?* My hands were trembling as I imagined a paralyzed girl being murdered. Even though Shante had tried to set me up, I wouldn't have wished death on her in return. I felt like her being stuck in the wheel chair was punishment enough. Now I had another death on my conscious.

I sat on the floor gripping the toilet trying to imagine DeMarcus committing a murder. The next second, he came through the door of the bathroom. I looked up at him. His eyes were bloodshot red, though still fine as hell, he didn't look like the same person I'd come to feel so strongly about.

"Did you really do that?" I asked.

"Yes," he said.

"Why?"

Staring down into my eyes he said, "Because I love you."

"What about your girlfriend?"

"I love *you*."

I didn't know how I was supposed to act. I did my best to stay numb for the entire weekend. As hard as it was, I forced myself to make small talk and try to be a good hostess to Harold and DeMarcus. I had mixed emotions. I fantasized about actually being free from any future criminal charges, but doubted it would be that simple.

I also realized that one of the things I'd like most about DeMarcus, his innocence, had been an illusion. I now looked at him like nearly every other man in my life. He was nothing more than another violent act waiting to happen. No different than Ali, Tony, or my father.

The next evening I left them all to go to work. It was strange but I actually looked forward to seeing the strangers. Compared to the one's I knew, the men who came into the club and handed over their money in exchange for the fantasy without possibility, were a relief. I knew nothing about them. It was better this way, them keeping their ugliness a secret.

At half past ten, as I was preparing to take the stage, someone took me gently by the arm. I turned around to see Jermaine, smiling.

"How you doin', lil mama?"

Don't know why but I hugged him. "Hey."

He embraced me back. "Damn, that's what's up. I appreciate that love."

Immediately, all eyes were on him. "You come to see me?"

"You could say that. It's my partner's birthday. He wanted to come over here and get a few drinks before we hit 112. But of course, I was hoping you'd be here. We've been here about an hour and we were getting ready to leave, but if you're about to do your thing, of course I'll stay and check you out. I don't want to make you uncomfortable though."

"Why, you've already seen me naked and you've..." I caught myself. I was about to remind him that we'd already fucked.

"Yeah, and *that* was nice. But remember I said that I wanted to be your friend."

"I remember.

"Friends don't sit around gawking at each other while they stripping."

"Suit yourself," I replied. "Your loss."

"So you don't mind me watching you dance then?"

"As long as you tipping, knock yourself out, brother."

Ten minutes later I was surprised to see him and his two friends sitting at the tables adjacent to the runway.

I strolled out in a lime green bikini bottom and a silver, studded, T-shirt that was cut-off at the midriff. As soon as Adina Howard's voice started blasting through sound system the show they'd been waiting for started. I reached the end of the catwalk and mouthed the words to the song as I began to grind my hips against the air. *'I need a roughneck nigga that will satisfy meeeeee'*.

I tried not to concentrate on Jermaine, but I wanted him to be impressed with my dancing. A spin here followed by a seductive wag of my big ol' butt and instantly, I could hear the men on my right yelling, "Damn," at the top of their lungs. A couple of fives floated onto the stage as I walked past.

Then as the song reached its' breakdown I started to rub my breasts through the material of my shirt. More money flew onto the stage as I went slowly from a handstand into a cartwheel. A second later, I'd landed in a split and was now eye to eye with Jermaine. The seduction had begun. It was all in fun for us as we smiled flirtatiously. He'd already experienced my pussy, but the look on his face made it clear he surely wanted more. He'd already given me money and a car, and I wanted more. Still, I didn't get the feeling that it was strictly about that for us.

It was as if we'd started all over. I grinned at him before I shifted my attention to the next man. His partner leaned in for a closer look and threw a twenty at me. He was drunk and obviously trying to compete with Jermaine. When I showed no reaction to the Jackson on the stage he pulled a handful of them out of his pocket and reached for me. His hand caressing my leg, he stuck bill after bill into my garter. He winked. I winked back. The fantasy was always for sale.

I stood up and moved to the other side of the stage. I couldn't ignore the patrons who only had ones to toss. I'd learned that they were the everyday customers. Make them feel special and they'd give you that same ten dollars every week forever.

When the song changed to Aaliyah's *Age Ain't Nothing But a Number,* I took my shirt off and while the intro played, I pranced slowly down the walk with my fingertips covering my nipples as if I was shy.

Then, as her angelic voice began, I got down on my knees and simulated being pushed onto my back. Hands now at my side, breasts exposed, I lifted my legs in the air and humped an invisible lover. I untied the strings of my bottom and tossed it behind me. My ass on display, the money began to flow. I worked each man seated by the stage and then stood at the end of the walkway as the men in the crowd came up to get a closer view of my coke bottle-like frame. Every single one of them whispered a weak line as they handed over the cash.

"I want to taste that."

"I'll pay whatever to fuck."

"Let me take you away from all this."

"You are soooo sexy."

"What time you get off?"

I'd heard it all before except for what Jermaine said as he handed me five one hundred dollar bills. "This is not your future. Call me tomorrow, baby." Then he headed for the door.

I was in the locker room counting my money. This nigga had made my night. It was only eleven o'clock and I had close to two thousand dollars.

I dialed his number. "Hello."

"This is me, Jayla."

"That was fast. I mean you calling me," he laughed.

"Yeah, I wanted to say thank you to you and your boys. You guys really made my night."

He laughed. "That was nothing. But you're welcome."

I didn't know what to say next so I blurted it out. "I have some people at my apartment from out of town, and I don't really want to be around them. I was wondering if I could hang out with you and your boys."

"That's for sho', showty. You know how to get to Club 112?"

"Yeah."

"Well when you get off, come on over. Call me once you get out front and I'll have someone bring you right in."

"Cool. I'll see you in an hour or so."

When I arrived at the club, I called his cell and as he promised, his partner came right to the door and got me. In VIP there were at least twenty women hovering around Jermaine and his boys. When he saw me he waved me over.

"Hey, everybody, this is my lil' sister, Jayla."

Sister?

"Hey, girl." From that moment on, I got nothing but love from every girl there. We drank bottles of Dom and laughed for the next three hours. I was shocked when he introduced me to a girl named Christine, who he said was his fiancé. She looked like a model and was sporting a huge rock on her finger that made me do a double take. She didn't stay long, but while she was there she didn't seem the least bit intimidated by all the women in his presence, which surprised me.

Jermaine, didn't like her hanging out. She seemed grateful for the time she'd had. He kissed her on the lips and told her he'd see her the next day. It was boy's night out. She scooted out of the club like a trained puppy.

When we left the club, it was like a rock star escaping through the back door of an arena. Women were disappointed that the show was ending without being chosen. After Christine had departed, he'd promised at least five of the women who'd been hanging around that he'd be leaving with them, but at four in the morning the only woman inside of his suite at the Ritz Carlton was me.

"I thought I was your sister," I said giggling.

"My sister from another mister," he laughed. "My friend…" he was drunk as hell. "My everything."

I didn't understand what was going on between he and I, but as he ate my pussy, I felt completely relaxed. Being with him had been like being on vacation from my life. I decided to enjoy him and not think about any of my worries.

A few minutes of his tonguing me and we started to get into a groove. The liquor had emboldened me and I grabbed him by the back of the head and locked him into a position that had him beating my clit with the perfect amount of pressure.

I closed my eyes and shook myself through an orgasm. I expected him to fuck me but instead he scooted up and began jerking his dick off. "Play with your titties," he instructed me.

I obliged him as he stroked his dick at a furious pace. "You look so sexy," I said.

"Yeah, talk that shit," he grunted.

I kept one hand on my left breast and stuck the other in my pussy and began to finger fuck myself. "You like this?" I asked.

"Oh, fuck yeah," he said. "Fuck that pussy with your fingers."

I was doing it to turn him on, but watching him jacking his meat off in excitement started to affect me. His eyes were fixed on me. I took my hand from my breast, licked my fingers and moved it to my clit.

Suddenly, it was no longer an act for me. I felt an orgasm coming. I'd never played with my pussy for a man before. "Ohhhh, shit, baby, I'm about to come."

"Come for me, baby," he said. "Come for me."

I did as I humped my hands and screamed out, "Yesssss, ooohhhhhhh, yesssssssss."

In the throes of my orgasm his body locked up and I felt the warm droplets of his sperm landing on my tits. He moaned out, "Ahhhhhhhhh," and aimed for my face. "Open your mouth, open your mouth."

The freak that I'd become, I did exactly what he asked. He leaned in and shot nut across my face, some landing on my tongue. I reached for his dick and jerked it a few times and leaned in, taking the tip in my mouth. "Ohhhhhh, yeahhhh," he moaned and then pulled it away. He fell to his back and told me quite simply, that I was the shit.

"There's a future for you with me. I'm keeping you around, the only way I know how," he said as he stared up at the ceiling.

"Friends?" I asked.

Mimicking the old Whodini song he finished with, "How many of us have them?"

Truth Hurts

Chapter 15

On Sunday Morning I walked back into the apartment and no one spoke a single word to me. I Ignored them right back and went straight to the bathroom and started running my bath water. Brandy knocked on the door and turned the knob at the same time. I was already in the tub soaking.

"Can I help you?" I asked.

"Nia, why you acting all crazy? I'm the one who got raped. Okay, so I didn't tell you they were coming, but is that any reason to leave DeMarcus here by himself like that? He came all the way down here for you. And what he did at home, he did for you."

"Brandy, first of all, I didn't tell him to do shit for me. You think I didn't have enough trouble with the law. Now he goes and does this shit, trying to be gangster. He killed a paralyzed bitch. Don't you get it?

On top of that, the last time I saw him, he wouldn't make love to me because he had a girlfriend. So what am I supposed to do somersaults now because he shows up?"

"I'm just saying…"

"You ain't saying shit. As far as I'm concerned he can leave, and forget about me ever coming back to D.C. They'll probably bury me underneath the fucking jail."

"So where did you go last night?"

"Why?"

"Because you've never spent the night out."

"I was with Jermaine."

Her face turned into a scowl. She walked out slamming the bathroom door.

A minute later another knock came. "Can I come in?" It was DeMarcus.

"Might as well and bring Harold with you."

"Huh?"

"Just come on in."

He walked through the door as I soaped up. His eyes locked on my breast. "Wow, I see you all tatted up."

"A little something."

"So, Nia, what's up with us? I mean I put it all on the line for you…"

"DeMarcus, I didn't ask you to do that."

"Right, and you didn't ask me to fight Tony that night for you in the club. I'm a man. A soldier and that's what we do."

"DeMarcus, I'm trying to figure out why you think it was so thorough for you to kill a crippled chick."

"That crippled chick could have gotten you twenty years, but I see how you rolling. You down here, catching baller after baller, so you don't need me." I didn't have a response as I digested his words. He went on, "I mean, who *are* you? What *are* you?"

"What do you mean?"

"I mean you're sitting up here acting like you don't want the drama, or to be a part of the violence, but all you do is run behind killers. I thought you wanted a gangsta, so I did what I thought you'd expect a gangsta to do."

I got up out of the tub. The water ran between my breast and off of my body. I nearly turned him to stone when he saw me naked and wet. I grabbed my towel. I walked into the bedroom. He followed me.

I reached for the lotion and started to rub it on my shoulders. "DeMarcus, I don't know why I'm acting like this.

I've been through so much in the last year. I've lost my father, my best friend, and my mother all in one year. I fell in love with you, but I had to leave you too. I don't think I ever loved Ali to be honest, but I did love what he did for me, financially and physically." I could tell he didn't like what I'd said but I had to get it off my chest.

I continued on staring directly into his eyes. "I could get picked up by the authorities tomorrow and who knows what would happen to me? I was so angry at my father for leaving me alone. I spent a whole year hating him for that, and now that I want to visit him and write him, I can't." The emotions were starting to take hold of me.

"I brought Brandy down here and she got hurt because of me. Ali is in jail because of me... and now you go and do this... because of me." My voice was cracking as I tried to get it all out. "DeMarcus... you're too good for this. You're too... good for me."

"What are you talking about? I love you. I'm not too good for you. You can't help the hand you were dealt." He leaned in and hugged me.

"No... you are. You have a bright future... just go home and forget about me. Never tell anyone what you did. You're smart, handsome... you can do anything you want in life... me... I'm... nothing..."

Before I could finish he was kissing me telling me that he loved me. I felt so dirty. All of my secrets, coupled with the fact that I felt like I'd become a whore. It was too much and I began to cry.

Still, I let him fuck me.

A few hours later we were still lying in the bed smoking some more of the haze. We'd just finished sharing a laugh

after listening to Brandy and Harold in the next room fucking
on the fold-out couch.

"I want you to come home," he said.

"I'm afraid."

He paused and said, "You don't want to come home do
you? I mean would you, if you could?"

I thought about it for a minute. "I'm not sure."

"You like it here that much?" he asked.

"DeMarcus, I hate my stepfather and everything at home
reminds me of Neek. Maybe I like being here because it's not
there."

"Don't you want to finish school, so you can..."

"I make nearly two grand a week at the club, I don't need
school...," I caught myself.

"You make what?" I'd slipped up and now he was staring
me in the face. "At what club?"

For some reason I just blurted it out, "I'm a dancer now.
I strip at a club."

It was as if I'd just thrown a bucket of water on him.
"Are you serious?"

"Yeah, I'm serious." I got up and pulled my bag out of
the closet and showed him a couple of outfits that were on the
top.

With look of astonishment he asked, "And you're proud
of that shit? I don't believe this."

Now I was offended with his tone. "Motherfucker, don't
judge me."

He shook his head and stood up. He started getting
dressed. "Fuck this. I give up. I did all this for you and you'd
rather stay down here, shaking your ass and spreading your
pussy for dollars?" he yelled. "Man, fuck this."

It was like déjà vu. Only now, he was the one stomping
out the door on me. He had his clothes on in less than a

minute. "Forget you ever met me. You're dead to me. Dead as Neek is to you."

That shit hurt me to my heart and I got up and took a swing at him. He caught my arm. "Only because you are Harold's cousin…" was all he said. I got the message that he would have hit my ass.

He walked out the bedroom door. "Harold, I'll be waiting in the car," he said as he picked up his backpack and the keys.

Harold looked at me, "Everything okay?"

I quickly stuck my head out of the room and said, "Drive safe, Harold," before going back in the room, and slamming the door.

One month later and Brandy's ass was throwing up on the regular. I had her pee on the stick to, more or less, confirm what we already knew. Five minutes after she'd taken the test the verdict was in. She'd let Harold bust nut after nut up in her and now she was knocked up.

"What the hell am I going to do?" she asked.

"What do you want to do?"

We sat on the couch watching the *Wayans Brothers* each of us eating out of our own tub of Ben & Jerry's. "I think I should find out what Harold wants."

"Harold's my family, but I'll be honest. It's your decision. What you do with your body shouldn't have anything to do with him. If you have it, no doubt, he'll affect how you raise the baby, but he shouldn't affect whether or not you have it. You have to be prepared to raise it on your own no matter what he says. Niggas get all excited at the idea of buying tiny-ass Air Jordan's and throwing a football around in the front yard, and then they run the fuck out on your ass. So it's about what you want to do."

"You're right."

We kept eating our ice cream. "Bitch, you know I love you, right?"

She laughed. "So will you be my baby's daddy?"

We laughed again. "I'm too young to be a daddy, but I'll be a godmommy."

For the first time in a while we enjoyed a normal couple of weeks. I hadn't heard from DeMarcus, which made me both nervous and sad. I was sad that I'd hurt him, and nervous thinking that he might want to see me in trouble. But now that he'd gotten blood on his hands, I didn't so much fear that possibility since he knew I could return the favor if he snitched.

Brandy had gone back to work at the club the week after Harold and DeMarcus left. We'd both been making plenty of money and doing a bunch of shopping.

When I wasn't at work or hanging out with Brandy, Jermaine and I were hanging out together almost constantly. He took me to Atlanta's best restaurants and we hit the clubs at least once a week. He kept introducing me as his little sister to everyone in his circle, then at the end of the evening we'd sneak off and later on in the hotel of his liking, he'd live out his perverted fantasies with me.

He won me over in spite of his shortcomings; the wifey at home and the little penis. Respected men were a turn on to me and Jermaine commanded it from everyone around him. On top of that he was hilarious and very charming. Our arrangement worked for me because I wasn't after anything serious after all that I'd been through, and he didn't try to take it there. He also knew how to treat a woman spoiling me with gifts and money. He never talked about Christine and she never seemed to call when we were together.

He still felt bad about what had happened with Brandy and tried to go out of his way to be nice to her. She remained apprehensive. "If you want to hang with him, go ahead," she said.

She spent so much of her time on the phone or sitting on the couch watching television. I started to worry about her and finally I sat down and begged her to let me know if she was okay.

Her response helped me put it all into perspective, "Nia, do you know that this is the first time in my life that I've been able to have shit that I don't gotta hide to keep from having it stolen. It's the first time I can actually sit and watch television or talk on the phone in peace. I'm in heaven here with you.

Have you forgotten the situation I was in? Back at home, our television sat in the pawn shop half the time and the cable got cut off more than it stayed on."

I decided to leave her alone after that conversation.

A couple of weeks later we were on the way to the club for work when Brandy turned down the radio and said, "Nia, I'm going to have the baby."

"Did you tell Harold yet?"

"I told him I was pregnant. He said he wants me to have it. He wants me to move home."

"What do you want? You can't live for someone else."

"I want to be happy."

I laughed. "Don't we all? But don't think a baby is going to bring you that. Or that a man will, for that matter."

"What do you think will?"

"Only you know that. Living your dreams, or at least chasing them, is a good start. Do you have any dreams?"

"Yeah, but it's not something I could ever do."

"What is it? And I don't want to sound like your second grade teacher, but you can do anything you want to, except become a singer. Your voice is horrible."

She laughed, "You know, I've always wanted to be a cheerleader. Like a Dallas Cowboy's cheerleader or a Laker Girl."

"Really? I never knew that."

"Yeah, that and I've also always wanted to have a baby and have someone to love me. Someone good, like Harold."

"Well, you can have those things. And you *can* be a Laker Girl. You're a hell of a dancer."

"Thanks, but I guess I'll settle for having a baby."

"And moving home?" I looked over at her. "You ready to do that?"

"I guess."

For a multitude of reasons her answer upset me. I was never one to be selfish, but the thought of losing the only family I had left, was a bitter pill to swallow. I felt like I'd done so much for her and that her willingness to leave showed a complete lack of gratitude.

Two days before my seventeenth birthday, Brandy left Atlanta with Harold and moved home. She was four months pregnant. I moved into a new apartment, changed my phone numbers and left Club Crystal. It was the last time she and I would speak.

New Years Eve 1999
Chapter 16

At six o'clock on the dot, I pulled my white CLK 430 into the garage underneath of my apartment building and unloaded my bags. Three thousand dollars worth of shopping and all I had were a few pairs of shoes, a belt and some underwear. The Dolce & Gabanna dress I was wearing, along with the fifteen thousand dollar mink that Jermaine had bought me back from New York was already hanging up in my closet. I was ready to see the stares and glares from all the hating-ass sistahs when I walked into the Grand Salon Ballroom at the Fox Theatre.

Jermaine's cousins, Sammy and Marvin Randall, had hired one of the nation's hottest party promoters, Tracye Stafford, from Ikon Entertainment, to put together what was being billed as the only proper way to bring in the new millennium on the East Coast. Big Tigger, from BET was hosting the show. Outkast, Ja Rule, and Monica, were all supposed to perform along with DJ Rico from Washington, D.C. A host of NBA stars from the Hawks and the Magic were coming along with several celebrities who'd made Atlanta their home, like Bobby Brown and Whitney. It was rumored that Puffy was in town and might be stopping through. The entire town was buzzing about the event, which had sold out in two days. There were rumors that the Randalls had screened who received the tickets and that this was going to be an all-beautiful-people, ATL A-list, extravaganza.

The girls at the new club I worked at knew I was tight with Jermaine and nearly every one of them begged me to get them tickets. They may as well have asked me for an organ.

The only girl I was bringing along was Destiny, who I'd remained close with, even after leaving Club Crystal for the Mirage. She was like a big sister to me, always giving me advice. She was into fashion like me, so we bonded over our constant trips to the mall. Destiny reminded me of a country version of Janet Jackson, except for the nose. Destiny had a stereotypical, spread-across-the-face, black person's nose. But she was cute as hell and soft spoken like Janet, and Michael, for that matter.

She and I had gotten tight after Brandy left, if for no other reason than I had no other woman around that I trusted. I even tried to get her to come with me to work at the Mirage, but she claimed she had it too good with Polo. I let her suit herself, but the money I was seeing was twice what I made at Club Crystal.

The Mirage was a premier club that didn't even allow lap dances. Instead the girls would do private shows in the champagne rooms for VIP. They weren't even allowed to touch you, yet they would lay two hundred down like it was nothing. I only danced a few nights a week and made more money than most of the girls in the city. The rest of my time I spent working out, shopping. I even read a book on the life Assata Shakur. Ali had bought it for me a while back and told me that I needed to put something in my head other than the magazines I routinely read. Then I read a few books about the modeling industry. I found them particularly helpful since I'd started taking some photographers up on their offers for photo shoots, during the past year. I learned enough to know that no matter what any of the photographers said about it helping my career, I didn't *have* to do any nude shots.

At first I was scared of having my pictures wind up on the internet, but with so many years gone by since I'd left D.C., I was beginning to lose any fears I had about still being sought after. There was no way I could be sure that I was in the clear, but I slept good at night. As bad as I wanted to, I hadn't made any direct contact with my mother, or anyone from home, in all this time. Still, I made it a point to send postcards to her whenever I was away from Atlanta. In case the authorities were looking for me, they'd see that I was in places like Houston, New Orleans and Miami.

I walked through the door of my apartment and set my bags down. I changed into my workout gear and jumped on the treadmill for twenty minutes, did crunches until my body hurt. Next, I shadow boxed along with Billy Blanks while I imagined knocking a chick's head off who'd gotten out of line. After a hot shower, I shut the lights off, spread my still-wet body out across the bed, and turned on some soft music so that I could take a power nap.

It seems as though I was just getting off to sleep good when my house phone began to ring. I lifted my head up and reached for the handset. "Hello," I said.

Click.

"No they didn't," I mumbled and sank my face back into my pillow.

It rang again five minutes later. This time I noticed that it was a blocked call. Still, I picked up. "Hello."

"Yeah, is this Jayla?"

"Who is this?"

"This is Christine."

I knew exactly who it was but I wanted to play her off. "Christine, who?"

"Jermaine's wife."

"His fiancé?"

"His wife," she repeated.

"Yeah, okay, what's up?"

"That's what I'm calling to ask you. I've been hearing that you and him, are more than friends. I know you aren't really brothers and sisters. I also know where you work."

"What about it?"

"I just want to know if you are fucking my man?"

I laughed. "Girlfriend, did you ask him?"

"No,"

Then I yelled into the phone, "Well... why the fuck are you on my phone? If you don't have the nerve to ask him this dumb shit, then why would you ask me? I'm the wrong bitch to fuck with on some dumb shit like this."

"You don't have to get hostile...I'm just."

"Bitch, you call here waking me up, hanging up, calling back. Fuck this. I'll fuck you up. I know where you work at too, ho."

I heard her voice cracking and I actually felt sorry for her. She had that deep-in-love, ready-to-kill-herself, pitiful tone, "Can you just tell me, please. If you are fucking him you can have him. I'll leave the picture..."

I thought about what she was saying. I didn't want her man, not *all* to myself. I loved being his friend. Yes, I did fuck him from time to time. I also did other things for him that he paid me quite well too, such as making deliveries, transporting weapons or money, and any other thing that popped into his mind. I wanted to tell her what she wanted to hear, but betraying him was not an option.

"Christine, I don't know what you heard, but Jermaine and I are only friends. I'm not fucking him. Please, don't call my phone with this again."

She was silent. "Did you hear me?" I asked.

She hung up.

160

The forty-foot, JumboTron was showing the ball about to drop in Times Square. The deejay turned the music down long enough for everyone to raise their glasses. I'd been in the party for an hour, sitting in a roped off section for the VIP of the VIP's. As usual there was a smorgasbord of dime pieces crowding around Jermaine, his boys, and his cousins trying desperately to be noticed.

The party was packed and was living up to everything that it had been hyped up to be. Ball players, gold diggers, rappers, video hos, actors, radio personalities, the dope boys, stick-up boys, feds and politicians were all partying together.

Destiny was having a blast, running back and forth to the dance floor. I wished I hadn't worn my fur coat and because I didn't want to set it down, I'd spent the last hour holding it.

"Eighteen, seventeen, sixteen…" I felt Jermaine grab my hand and pull me off the couch I was sitting on. "Ten, nine, eight…"

"Hold your glass up, quick…put your coat right there," he yelled.

"Four, three, two…" The room erupted. "HAPPY NEW YEAR." Then I felt a torrent of liquid being sprayed landing on my face. Every nigga within fifty feet had bottles of Cristal exploding into the air. My dress was soaked. Jermaine grabbed me and kissed me on the mouth.

"Happy New Year, Nia," he said. He was one of two people in Atlanta who knew my real name. I'd come to trust him fully.

His drunken kiss was soft and lingering. When I pulled away he smiled and said, "Don't worry about that dress." He pulled a stack of money out of his pocket and peeled off a stack of hundreds. "Put that away."

I didn't count it before I tucked it in my purse. "Let's go dance," he said.

"What about my coat?" He turned to one of his friends.

"Ernie, watch her coat. That mink right there." Ernie nodded. "C'mon, let's go bring this year in right." Jermaine held a bottle of champagne in one hand as had started dancing right there. We passed the bottle back and forth chugging its' contents like Kool-aid.

We hit the floor as *Celebrate* by Kool and the Gang played. He was so silly, doing all the old school dances, bringing a bunch of attention to himself. He started doing the running man, then the cabbage patch, followed by a few that were before my time. He was a good dancer though and not one to be outdone, I started giving him a run for his money, even as my head began to spin from the alcohol.

He got all up on my ass and I threw it at him without hesitation. I spun, shook and worked my body as if I was trying to win a contest. Before I knew it all of his boys were on the floor and we were like a party within the party. We kept it going for almost twenty minutes as DJ Rico, played songs from way back.

When *Heartbeat* by Taana Gardener came on, the crowd went off. It was a sexy song from back in the late seventies. I had used it at the club to dance off of. So when I started to really get my groove on, the crowd formed around me. With Jermaine still in front of me, I started playing with the straps on my dress, sliding them off my shoulder.

He started howling and the crowd around us began to part ways as if a fight had broken out. Next he began to hold up hundred dollar bills and I smiled. I pushed my hands up to the air as if to say 'raise the roof', but what I meant was it was going to take more than a few hundreds to see me set it off.

He moved up to me and stuffed a G into my bra. I let the shoulders drop and kept dancing, leaning back, until I could see the person behind me. When I came back up, he handed me another wad of cash and I let the dress fall to the floor. It was already soaked in bubbly so I said what the hell. The crowd erupted as my La Perla lingerie was now on display. The lace bra and thong sent the place into a roar.

I continued dancing as if I was fully dressed and Jermaine did as well. When the next song came on and I saw the smile on his face I knew that he'd been behind it. He held the bottle of Cris to my mouth and I drank down a few more gulps.

'36-24-thirtayyy-sixxx what a winning hand, cause she's a brick house...'

I gave him the show he wanted and danced seductively for the next couple of minutes. It was as if I was part of the show, helping to ensure that this party would be talked about for months to come. I saw the men gawking and the women looking on in both disgust and envy. Once the deejay mixed another song in, I stopped dancing. Bending over, I picked my dress up and I headed for the VIP to gather my coat.

"Jermaine, I'm going to go home and get another dress."

"What for?"

"Because this one is soaked with liquor and it's been on the nasty ass floor."

"Okay. It won't take you too long will it."

"Nah, I'll be right back. Keep your eye on Destiny for me though, I'ma leave her here."

"She's fine. I think my boy, Mo is sweet on dat azz."

"I'm sure." Mo was his three hundred pound friend who'd played for the Falcons before being injured two years earlier. Now he was the equivalent of a bodyguard.

Clad only in my fur, I took off through the crowd. My apartment was only ten minutes from the party and since it was only one A.M., it was too early for me to spend the rest of the night in my bra and panties.

I made it to the front door and saw the long line. I motioned for Big Lenny, who was making a fortune doing security, charging people with no I.D.'s an extra hundred a pop. "Make sure my spot is still here for me," I said.

"Sure thing, baby. How long you gone for?"

"Just running up the street to the house, I spilled something on my dress."

He laughed as I opened my fur and showed him that I was in my bra. "Jayla, you a mess." He pointed to a car that was just in front of the door. "When you get back, pull up in that spot."

"Okay." I headed off and as I made my way through the parking lot I heard a voice that had alarming familiarity, not just the voice, but the accent. It wasn't southern, at least not Atlanta southern.

"Nia," the voice called. "Nia, is that you?"

I looked over and saw a man standing at the end of the line who looked familiar. Chocolate skinned, a five o'clock shadow, bright white teeth and an inch-long, neatly-trimmed, Afro.

"Nia, it's me," he said as I had gotten closer to him. It was just dawning on me that this brother knew my real name. Once I reached him I stopped.

"Ivan," I said.

He smiled and reached for me. We hugged and my coat fell open. I pulled away quickly and closed it with my hands. "That's quite an outfit you got on there."

"A long story. I spilled something on my dress." It was balled up and stuffed inside my purse.

"So, you living down here or are you just here to party?"

"Both," I laughed. As we stood there my mind took me back home. "What about you?"

"I came down here to go to Morehouse, but I hooked up with some folks down here that are into the music industry. I started making some beats and now I'm going at it full time. My mother was pissed that I dropped out of school with only a year left, but I had to follow my dreams."

"I didn't know you were into music like that."

"Yeah, I wasn't when we met. Back home in D.C. it wasn't something that I really talked about. As a kid I played the keyboard, but once I got older and started running with Tony and a few others, I kind of abandoned it."

The mention of Tony, chilled me. "So is it going well for you?"

"Actually it is. I've sold beats to a bunch of people. I actually just finished something for a deejay right here from Atlanta. He's a really good rapper. I got a feeling the kid is about to blow up, his name is Chris. Watch out for him."

"That's hot. You sound excited about what you're doing."

"Yeah, I'm loving it. So it looks like you're done for the night, huh?"

"No, I'm running home to change and I'm coming back." Getting caught up in the conversation, I invited him, but conventional wisdom would have me blame all the liquor I'd ingested. "You wanna ride with me. When we get back, you won't have to wait in line."

He looked over at a couple of guys in line, "I got a couple of friends with me."

"They'll still be in line when we get back. But it's on you."

He walked over to them and said a couple of words. A second later we pulled off in my car.

"This is nice," he said. "I actually drove one of these before I purchased my car."

"What do you have?"

"Jaguar XK8. I just copped it a couple of months ago, traded my Vette for it."

"You must be making some really good beats."

He laughed. "I'm doing okay. But look at you. You've grown all the way up. You were always pretty and ...developed," he laughed out, "But what you got going on right now. You looking like you need to be doing some magazine covers. Shit," he exclaimed.

"Thank you sir."

We arrived at my apartment and he went up with me. He gave me a boatload of compliments on the décor. Jermaine had picked it all out and had it delivered from North Carolina.

"You smoke?" I asked as I handed him one of the twenty pre-rolled, J's, I had in a box on the coffee table.

"Every now and then, but hell it's New Year's." I lit it and passed it to him. I was seated next to him in nothing but my lingerie.

A few puffs and I was feeling super relaxed and way too comfortable. I said, "Ivan, do you ever think about what happened back home? Neek, Tony, Shante?"

He looked me in the eyes and said, "Every single day." He took a pull of the weed. "It used to make me sad, but now I use it as motivation. I'm thankful that it wasn't my life. Tony could have dragged me down."

"What about Neek?"

"I miss her, but honestly, sometimes it feels like it was so long ago. But every so often, a song will come on, or when I'm home in D.C., I'll drive past the block and I'll stop to wonder how things might have turned out. How long we would have lasted."

I looked over at him and looked at how he'd matured. He was a year older than me I remembered. So at twenty-one, he

166

was turning into one hell of a man. I skipped the subject. "I can't believe you, of all people, would stop going to school. All you talked about was education. It was almost weird how much you loved school back then. I think you should finish."

"You sound like my mother," he said. "I will. One day, I will."

"Let me get dressed so we can head back." I went back into the bedroom, laid out another outfit, and hopped in the shower.

I was careful to not get my hair wet while I soaped my body down. As the steam filled the room, I looked at the door of the bathroom and Ivan was standing there. I was slightly startled, but not because he could see me naked, but because he too, was completely nude.

"Can I get in?" he asked.

I looked at him and my mind went rushing back to memories of Neek and him. She loved him. He was her first and her only. "Ivan this isn't why I brought you here."

Still standing there he responded, "I believe you." Then he moved closer to the shower door waiting for my approval.

I nodded 'yes' and said. "Fuck it, it's New Years Eve," as I opened the door.

In With the New
Chapter 17

Ivan and I went back to the New Year's party and I got him and his friends in with me. They'd been in line praying that they would eventually make it in. When they breezed inside with me without paying they were beyond excited. They all wanted to buy me drinks, which I declined because I drank for free in VIP. I did however promise Ivan a dance. Unfortunately, I didn't see him again for the rest of the night because the party wound up getting shut down by the police when three people were shot in the parking lot a little after three in the morning.

"You okay," Jermaine kept asking me after I'd returned.

I was fine but still stunned that I'd had sex with Ivan. He had rocked my world in a way that I hadn't in a while. He had a nice touch and soft lips. On top of that, he was blessed with a nice-sized dick, super thick and not too long. Best of all, the nigga took charge like a real man.

I think that what was more mind-blowing was the rush of emotions I'd experienced. I'd actually cried during the sex. I was still tripping off of that. It was crazy but making love to Ivan made me feel closer to Neek.

Unable to shake the thoughts of her, my mind drifted back to days when things were better. Even though I attempted to stay in a party mood, I spent the rest of the night reflecting on the last four years of my life.

A little after ten o'clock the following morning, Destiny and I headed down to South Beach, along with six of Atlanta's most popular dancers, for *Black Out Magazine's* Battle of the Exotic Entertainers. It was a good thing that I loved the open road because we were in for a ten hour trip.

I'd heard rumors that the show was going to be filmed for an HBO special. I'd set aside a blonde wig and colored contacts for that reason. I could care less about winning the competition. It was a free trip, a free room, it was only topless, and I was getting paid so I was happy to go.

The whole ride I talked a hole in Destiny's head. After explaining what had happened between Ivan and me, she was like, "So... what's the problem again, bitch?' She laughed. "Cause I'm not comprehending this shit. You said the nigga is fine, talented and paid... and he fucked you good?"

"It's more than that."

"So it's all about the fact that he was with your best friend back home, right?"

"I guess."

Destiny was eating sunflower seeds and spitting shells into a cup as if her mouth was a machine made to do that. "Don't think for a minute that she would care if you got with him now. If you think he can make you happy for a day, a month or a year then go for it. It's like keeping that dick in the family and that dough," she laughed.

"You think so?"

"If she could she'd tell you to go for it. If it was the other way around what do you think she'd have done? Or if things were reversed and you were up there looking down, wouldn't you want her to give it a try?"

It was a weird way to look at things, but I rolled with it. "I guess I would."

"Well then. Have fun."

Destiny had a way of schooling me and helping me find my way when things got complicated. I was glad to have her

169

as a friend. For the next few hours we talked about everything from stripping to life-after-stripping. Destiny was twenty-six already and she made sure that she wouldn't be dancing in her thirties.

She wanted to own a few successful businesses like the Laundromat. After that she said she'd focus on meeting a retired athlete.

"They don't get as much attention, but most of them still have plenty of money. With them pot-bellies and graying hair, they love getting attention from a bad bitch. Two weeks in and they're taking you to meet momma. Next thing you know they think they've married a little career girl. You think *I'm* going to tell the nigga I shook ass for cash?"

I was cracking up. The fact was she was right made it even more hilarious. Dancers knew better than most women how to make men fall in love. We did it night after night, with different men.

By the time we reached I-95 at Palm Beach, Destiny was knocked out sleep. I listened to *Mary* with the top back while the Florida sun beat down on my head. It was seventy degrees and getting warmer the further south I drove. I found my mind drifting to thoughts of Ivan and I wanted to call him. I hadn't given him my number but had promised to reach out to him soon. I thought since it was only the next day, the call would be too soon.

Instead I called Jermaine. "Hey, man."

"What's going on, shawty?"

"I'm on the road to Miami."

"Oh, yeah. The HBO thing, right? I forgot all about that. You still driving?"

"We didn't leave until ten."

"So did you have a good time last night?" I thought about Ivan.

"Yeah, I did."

"You were off the hook. Everybody was talking about you stripping. I told them motherfuckers Lil' Kim don't have shit on you."

I laughed out. "Well I need to see some Lil' Kim money."

"In due time, baby," he said. "So what time is the taping?"

"Six tomorrow."

"Don't be surprised if you see me."

"I will be. So call first," I shot back.

"I know you don't have another one of your niggas down there."

"Maybe," I said. I had no one, but I never let him know when, or if, he was the only one tapping the box. Plus, after my night with Ivan, I wasn't sure he would be alone for long.

This was the fifth annual *Black Out Magazine* Miss Exotic Dancer competition. The magazine had been a largely underground hit for years, but now people were starting to jump on the bandwagon. The cable exposure could really cause the magazine, which focused the impact of sex and the Hip-hop culture, to blow up.

A few rappers had been open with the stories detailing their sexual encounters with groupies. It also had reports of men who'd claimed to have slept with some of the industry's most hardcore rappers. The spreads usually always featured the hottest strippers in the country, or some wannabe models, who'd resorted to showing all of their ass in magazines like *KING, Smooth, XXL* and *Black Men* in order to get their faces out there.

Destiny went on first and did a great job in the one-on-one phase of the competition against a dancer named Storm from St. Louis. I watched on the monitor in the back as Destiny, clapped her ass cheeks and sent the crowd into a frenzy. She would win the competition hands down if she kept doing that.

I dogged a girl from Houston. It didn't take much more than my walking down the platform. She was butt ugly and had no tits. The first few rounds were a joke.

Once the final twelve dancers were introduced and brought onto the stage, I almost fainted when I looked across from me and saw the girl on the end. She was from the Nation's Capital and her name was Jazzy.

"Damn, she looks familiar," I said aloud.

We had a ten minute break and I sat in a chair the entire time trying not to stare at Jazzy. It was hard. She had me in awe at her flawless skin, banging weave. Remembering the buck teeth, I wondered how much money had been spent to equip her with such a beautiful smile. She definitely was sporting the finest tits money could buy, and in her bikini was an ass like a track star that surely had to come from implants too.

I was dumbfounded and my poor concentration caused me to catch an L in the next round. It was cool with me because Destiny ended up in the finals competing against Jazzy and one other girl, Dior. Jazzy had moves like no other, and had most of the men in attendance mesmerized, but Destiny's booty bounce landed her second place, with Dior taking first.

Dior was a crowd favorite, having been in thirty music videos and gaining notoriety from being video taped by one of L.A.'s top rappers giving him head, and had too much buzz not to win.

Once the competition was over we changed clothes. Destiny was headed to Wet Willie's with a couple of the girls she knew from Atlanta. I told her that I was tired, "I'll pass."

"You sure?"

"Absolutely. That drive was something and someone fell asleep on me."

She chuckled, gave me a hug, and told me she'd call me when she got in. We both prepared to head out the door on to Ocean Drive. As I'd hoped, I saw Jazzy walking out the door. Curiosity was getting the best of me so, I walked up and grabbed her arm. "Excuse me, but you look so familiar."

She was facing me and smiled. "I should, you've known me all your life."

"Say what?"

"You might remember me as Jasper," she laughed and continued, "Buck-tooth Jasper." I was in shock and my mouth dropped wide open. "Yes, Nia, it's me."

We had a lot to talk about. Jasper, who was now Jazzy, sat in my hotel room and we talked well into the night. Julie, my mother's best friend, still lived in our old apartment. I was happy to hear that Julie and Jasper had remained close even after he'd confessed his desire to live his life as a woman to her years back.

"You know, Brandy told me that you and she had gotten close before she left."

"Yeah, I had just worked up the nerve to tell her, but she up and vanished into thin air. I think she suspected it, why else would Miss Gorgeous have spent so much time hanging out with me?"

"Well, I don't know. She's a little gullible. She told me that you had really changed. I guess she had no idea how much." I laughed thinking about it.

We kept talking while we popped the drinks in the cabinet. The last he'd seen my mother, she seemed okay but never the way she was growing up. My leaving had hurt her. Jasper told me the details of some of his sexual experiences. He worked in a club in Southwest, D.C., and said he loved his penis but wanted a pussy. He really wanted to be respected as a woman, so I made a mental note to try. I'd refer to him as *her* from now on.

I needed to smoke and went into my stash. "Let's go on the balcony and hit this," I said.

Jazzy said, "If you want to get high, you need some of this." She pulled out a glass container full of weed.

"What the hell is that?"

"This is how they sell it down here. I got it from a guy I know out in Opa-Locka. I'm telling you, this shit is the bomb. The real hydro."

"Well roll that shit up," I said. We were out on the balcony smoking and I was starting to realize that the weed Jazzy had was strong than a motherfucker. I was watching her lips move, but I couldn't hear a word she was saying.

At one A.M. my phone rang, "Yeah?"

"Guess who's here? What's your room number?"

"No you ain't," I said.

"Girl, gimme the damn room number."

"628."

He continued to talk until he knocked on my door. I opened up and there Jermaine was looking like a million dollars. "What's goin' on? You know I love South Beach," he announced. Then he looked over at Jazzy. "Who's your friend?"

"This is Jazzy."

"How you doin', Miss Jazzy."

"Fine. A pleasure to meet you."

He inhaled. "Ya'll in here getting high?"

We were already high and started laughing, "Uhhhmm," we said together.

"Well, don't hide it, divide it," he said.

We walked back out onto the balcony and lit up another couple of J's. "This shit is … this some good shit," he said. "Where you get this?" he asked.

"This is Jazzy's shit. She got it down here."

Jazzy chimed in, "This is some Jamaican Redbud, it's hydroponically-formulated," she laughed out. "Serious though, that's what my connect tells me when he charges me one fifty for a half ounce of this shit."

Jermaine pulled out two hundred dollars and said, let me get the rest of it. Jazzy looked shocked. I shrugged my shoulders, it was nothing new seeing him throw around chump change like that.

He kept smoking and began tossing back the bottles of liquor in the cabinet. "I'm loving this," he said, talking about the weed as if it was a person. Next, he started on about the party the previous night and how live it was. The more he smoked the more he talked.

I knew he was high out of his mind when he started complaining about Christine. He never talked about her to me. "I'm so tired of this bitch. She's so boring. She doesn't make me happy."

A half an hour later he was the only one still smoking and talking. I was stuck deep in a fog like no other. The weed had me on my back. Once he announced that he was staying in my room and that he wanted us to all go shopping in the morning he went out into uncharted territory.

"Hey, Jazzy," he said. "How much would you charge me if I wanted to see you eat, Nia's pussy?"

"Excuse me?" Jazzy gave him a disapproving look.

"C'mon, don't give me all that. I'm rich. I want to see you eat her pussy."

"I don't care about your money. You need to…"

"Fuck that. I'm high as hell, I got a pocket full of money and I want to see some freaky shit." He pulled out at a lump of cash and threw it at Jazzy. "Come on, now. Nia don't give a fuck, whatever makes daddy happy, she's down for it."

I listened to him. He sounded like a complete pig, as if he thought he owned me. I hid it but I didn't like his arrogance. Jazzy looked at me and I smiled. Jazzy scooped up the cash and tucked it into her pocket and scooted between my legs. She gave a tug on my Baby Phat sweats and pulled them down.

I wasn't nervous, instead for the first time, I felt used. Maybe because it didn't feel like a choice, maybe because, Jermaine, for the first time, insinuated that I'd been bought and paid for.

All of that went away momentarily as Jazzy's tongue caressed my thighs. Even with my senses dulled from the alcohol and the powerful weed, I felt the warmth of her tongue invading my folds. I looked over at Jermaine who had a half smile on his face indicating his satisfaction with what he was witnessing. All he needed was a pipe hanging from his mouth and a silk smoker's jacket to complete the picture of his Hugh Heffner fantasies.

"Eat that shit, that's right. Ya'll look so sexy," he said.

When Jazzy hit my clit, a shock caused me to tremble. I couldn't help the fact that I loved getting my cunt licked. Thanks to Brandy, years earlier, I'd learned that a man or a woman could do an excellent job of it. At the present, I had a little of both doing it.

I worked hard to get the images of Jasper out of my mind while I let Jazzy do her thing, treating my pussy like a frozen treat, licking the edges carefully as if she was trying to melt me. If I hadn't been so fucked up I would have never made the next suggestion.

I stopped myself from panting and yelled out, "Suck his dick."

Jazzy stopped and we both stared at Jermaine. He stood up and walked confidently over to us. He dropped his pants and without hesitation, Jazzy deep throated his undersized dick. "Oh, shit."

It didn't take long before Jermaine began to pant. Jazzy was obviously better at giving head to a man than to a woman. I found myself taking mental notes at her style. She tickled the head of his dick with her lips, sucked the tip and jerked him at the same time.

"Ohhhhh, yeaahhhh," he said. No longer able to stand, he collapsed onto the couch, stepped out of his pants and waited for Jazzy to continue with his pleasure.

At first, I was laughing on the inside, knowing what he didn't, but then as I continued watching him being swept along toward ecstasy, I began to get turned on. I lifted Jermaine's shirt and began to kiss and rub his chest.

"Ya'll bitches driving me crazy," he moaned. He was huffing and puffing while Jazzy gave him the blow job of a lifetime. When he started to lose control, I pulled away from his chest. "Oh shit, I'm about to…"

With out warning I heard his voice raise three octaves as Jazzy jammed a finger deep into his rectum. "Ahhhhhhh," he cried out.

Still sucking the tip, and jerking him with one hand, I watched in amazement as she fucked his asshole with her finger. His voice was like a siren as he began to bust his nut on Jazzy's face and in her mouth.

She licked him clean and pulled her finger out of his ass. I was shocked and alarmed that he'd gotten off like that.

Jazzy looked at me and winked. "I'm going down to my room to get cleaned up."

"Yeah, sure thing."

"I'm in 704," she said. "It's been a pleasure, Jermaine."

Still reeling from his climax he extended his hand. "Yeah," was all he said.

I went to sleep. When I woke up at six in the morning, Jermaine wasn't in my room. Jazzy surprised me when she called and told me that Jermaine was in her shower. "Girl, I just wanted to know what was up with you two. It seems like you have a pretty open relationship, but I didn't want you to think that I was trying to go behind your back."

At around four he'd knocked on her door and begged to come in. The rest was history. I was through a minute into what she began to describe as the salad-tossing, butthole-reaming, experience. By five A.M., Jermaine had discovered her cock but didn't seem to care. I stopped her short from giving me all the details of what went on. Didn't have the stomach for it.

By the time Jermaine came back to the room, I was out on the beach with Destiny. He caught so much shade from me the rest of the day that he couldn't have gotten a tan if he tried.

I decided to call Ivan after that. We had a great discussion as I laid out in the sun. We got a better chance to catch up and he asked if he could see me when I got back to Atlanta.

I asked, "For what?"

"It's not obvious?"

"That you want to fuck me again?"

"No, that I want to spend time with you. I think you're smart, sexy and the fact that you're from home... I like that."

I watched the waves rolling in the distance. I loved the ocean. "So let me ask you this…"

"Shoot."

"What do you want from me?"

"Can I be honest with you?"

"Please."

"Are you sure? It might upset you a bit."

"Go ahead."

"The day I met Neek, I was really taken by you. I wanted you from that minute, but I thought you were out of my league. I did come to really like Neek, but I never got over what I felt for you. Never. The day I saw you in the mall so long ago… I wanted to tell you then, but it was too soon. I thought I'd get another chance, way before now to tell you, but life has a way of letting things get done in its' own time."

"Wow."

"Do you know what I said when I saw you the other night?"

"Uhhh, nope."

"I said, there goes my wife. There goes the woman I'll be with forever."

It was a beautiful thing to say, but I thought that I should tell him the truth about me now, which would surely burst his bubble. "Ivan, I'm an exotic dancer. I strip. That's how I survived when I left D.C."

He laughed and said, "Are you serious? That's hot." When I was quiet he went on, "Was that supposed to discourage me? I don't give a damn bout' that. I'm digging you… all over again."

I saw Jermaine approaching and I said, "Let me call you back in a few minutes."

"Everything okay?"

"Everything is fine," I said and hung up.

As Jermaine stopped in front of me, I realized that I'd have to do without him and everything his money brought to my life. He'd made me feel cheap the night before. Then he proved himself to be suspect as far as his dealings with Jazzy. HIV was out there. I couldn't take those types of risk. So at that minute, I made a choice.

It was January the second, the second day of the new millennium, which to me amplified the meaning of one of the saying, *'out with the old... in with the new.'*

Playing Your Game
Chapter 18

It became apparent to me that Jermaine was up to no good when my phone rang at three o'clock in the morning, on Valentine's Day. The voice of desperation caught me totally off guard. "Bitch, I'm going to kill myself and these kids because of you."

Christine was starting up again. Her voice was more frantic this time. "What?"

"You're fucking my husband, I know it. Someone told me that he bought you a new car and moved you into the house out in Stone Mountain. If I knew where it was, I'd come out there and burn it down with you in it."

"Christine, wait a minute," I said in a whisper. I sat up in the bed, "It's not like that. It's not me."

"Don't lie to me, you black bitch. I know you're a whore. Don't lie to me," she screamed at the top of her lungs, clearly a woman over the edge.

I slid out of the bed and headed toward the door of my bedroom. I looked back at Ivan. He turned over but didn't wake up. I crept into the kitchen and took a seat at the breakfast bar. I was trying to keep my voice down. "Christine, I can prove to you that it's not me, but I have an idea who he's seeing, but you have to promise me that you won't do anything to yourself or your kids. I can talk to him and ..."

"Fuck you. You're gonna pay," she said and hung the phone up. She was clearly losing it.

At five o'clock I later that day I pulled up at Club Crystal and walked inside. Big Lenny had been waiting for me. We walked over to the side of the club where the pool tables were located so that we could talk in private.

Lenny was a stand up guy. He'd called me and told me that he had some information for me that he thought I might want to hear. He got me a drink and we racked the balls up.

Jermaine had been acting strange as of late and Lenny had noticed. "He keeps asking me about you, your past. Wanted to know exactly what I knew about you," Lenny said. "I asked if you two had a problem. He assured me everything was cool. But he kept saying that he wasn't sure if he could trust you."

"That's strange, because there's some weird shit going on with him that freaked me out and after the phone call I got from Christine, it's all starting to add up."

I told him about what happened in Miami. Big Lenny looked at me as if he was about to loose his lunch.

I broke it all down for Big Lenny. Told him that I had planned to cut Jermaine off anyway, but he'd beaten me to the punch. And how, at the time, I still didn't think Jermaine knew that I was aware of his ongoing exploits with Jazzy, at least to the best of my knowledge. But that all of a sudden, my phone calls went unanswered and my messages unreturned. With all of this I began to wonder.

As it turned out, my suspicions were warranted. Together Lenny and I figured out that Jermaine had to know that I was up on his dirty little secret. He knew because he and Jazzy were now some kind of item and it was a sure bet that she'd told him that we'd shared a long history.

Once Big Lenny added the reasons for his beef, everything became totally clear. "I had been trying to reach the nigga in regards to some business. When I got him on the line, he'd rushed me off the phone and told me he'd meet me later on that night because he was out of town. It just so happened that I was driving by the soul food spot that his uncle owns, down by Clark."

"Yeah, I know it," I said nodding my head.

"Well, I look up and he was on his way out the door with a bag of food. I circled back and drove past again. He didn't even see me, but he had a bitch with him. Big titties, falling out her shirt, a tight leather jacket and a phat onion. Any other time he goes out of his way to show off his women. When I called him back, he told me that he and his new lady, Jazz, were furniture shopping, so the next day would be better." I was so pissed that he was blowing me off that I told him I'd seen him earlier. "I haven't been able to get him on the phone since."

After hearing Big Lenny's bits and pieces of info, I realized that Jazzy was the one he'd purchased a car for, a 1999, red Corvette, no less. I imagined them cruising around, listening to Prince, while she gave him head, or vice versa. Of course, it didn't take much to figure that Jazzy was undeniably the one he'd moved into the same house where Brandy had been raped.

"So what do you think about all this, Lenny? How do you see it playing out?"

"I think, he's a faggot and now that he's in love with this Jazzy, he wants to cut us off. I think we need to get ours. Finish what Ali started years ago."

"You mean rob him? That was Frank Money."

"Actually it wasn't." He sat down and said. "Ali never wanted to rob Frank. He wanted Frank to lead him to Jermaine, which he did. He was going to rob Jermaine and kill everyone in the house. Including you and Brandy."

"What?"

"You knew that and you…"

"I didn't really know you then. He was going to pay me a nice cut to keep my mouth shut. I'd told him that he didn't have to kill you two, but he insisted no witnesses." I thought for a second how cold Ali was. He would have killed us. And I'd made it a point to send him money orders every month without fail as if it was my cable bill. Lenny went on, "Jermaine was worth hundreds of thousands back then. Now he's sitting on millions, I bet."

"So if we rob him, then what… we gonna sit around here and spend the money? You don't think he's gonna suspect us."

"Not if he's dead."

I sat back shook my head. Not again. "Lenny, I've just started feeling like I can have a life. I'm not interested in a murder beef."

"Well, I suggest you get out of town. Because I'm going to do it and his cousins are going to look at everyone who he's close to. There's a short list and you'd have to be on it."

I shook my head. "Lenny… you ever killed someone?" He didn't respond. "I didn't think so."

At first there was an intense look on his face. It gave way to the statement. "There's a first time for everything."

"This ain't the work for an amateur. Sorry, but you're playing by yourself on this one. I don't want any part of it. I'll survive without Jermaine. I hope he lives happily ever after. I'll tell you who you should call, his fiancé, Christine. She'd be glad to help you, I'm sure."

Lenny shook his head to show his disapproval at my unwillingness to participate in his scheme. "Like it or not, you're in the game. You might as well get paid."

"I don't think so," I said as I headed for the door.

Five days later, I was in the studio with Ivan. He was working on a track for a new girl group out of New Orleans. I had the TV on as I sat on the couch in the lobby waiting for him to finish so we could make love and work up an appetite. The music was playing through the speakers and the beat was so hot that I got up and started dancing. With all that was going on my life it was strange to me how I felt good whenever I was around Ivan, almost worry free.

He worked until a little after ten P.M. and we were about to head home when my cell phone rang. It was Lenny. I didn't answer, but he called back six times back to back. "Somebody wants you really bad," Ivan said.

"I know but..." it began ringing again. Finally I said, "Yeah, Lenny."

He sounded as if he was in the middle of fucking, he was out of breath, "Do you have the news on?"

"No, why?"

"Quick, turn on Fox 5. Quick." His tone got me excited and I grabbed the remote and changed the channel.

As soon as I did there was the reporter in front of a McDonald's in Stone Mountain. I watched and listened in amazement as the reporter gave details of a domestic situation gone terribly wrong. A twenty-five year old woman from Buckhead had just gone on a shooting rampage inside of the restaurant.

Christine's picture flashed on the screen and the reporter went into the breaking story. *At around eight o'clock this evening, Christine Walker, shot her estranged lover, Jermaine Randall four times in the chest, killing him in front of a dozen people. She also shot his companion, who has been identified as Jasper Davison, once in the head. Witnesses say she then walked to her vehicle where she shot her own children, ages two and four, before she turned the weapon on herself.*

A grisly scene here, as five people have been pronounced dead at the scene.

I was completely stunned. Big Lenny snapped me out of it. "Jayla, we have to go to that house. Can you remember how to get us to that house? I know there's money in that house."

"Do you know how long it's been since we were there?"

"You got to try."

"I'm with my man right now. I'll see what I can do."

He sounded like a drug addict begging for a hit of dope. "Please, call me back. Otherwise, the police or the bank or... somebody is going to get the money."

I knew of at least two other places where Jermaine probably kept money and drugs. I could have given Big Lenny those addresses but I didn't trust him anymore. He'd waited too long to tell me about Ali's plan to kill me.

I mourned Jermaine for all of five minutes as Ivan and I drove out to Stone Mountain. I shared only with Ivan the information that I felt he needed, explaining to him that he was about to be set if things went our way. "Twenty percent, of what we find is yours. That's simply for watching out."

If no alarm went off when I broke into the house, we'd be able to take our time and the sky was the limit.

He was so nervous as the schoolboy in him became so apparent. Schoolbooks and beats were all Ivan knew and I loved that about him. If I'd have taken Big Lenny, I wasn't sure that I'd walk out of the house with my life, let alone any cash.

Surprised at how sharp my memory was, I was able to drive straight to the house. Once there, we parked two houses away and walked back to Jermaine's. There was a light on in the basement so I walked up to the front door and rang the doorbell. If someone was in the house, we'd have to abort. I rang for a couple of minutes and when no one came, I breathed the first sigh of relief.

I moved to the back of the house and signaled for Ivan to come with me. We used a brick wrapped in a towel first to test for the alarm. A crash and a thud and the brick landed on the floor of the laundry room. No alarm. We took our time after that knocking out the glass so that I could open the latch to the window and lift it.

I climbed through and walked to the garage door and opened it. I noticed that the television was still on. A bag of weed was on the table next to an ashtray full of roaches. Maybe Jermaine and Jazzy had just gone to the McDonald's to satisfy a quick case of the munchies. It was a trip that turned out to be way more costly than a number five, super-sized.

"It's all good," I said as Ivan walked in.

We went through closets, cabinets, cut mattresses, moved beds out of the way and began to pull up carpet. An hour and half later we still hadn't found a thing. "Maybe he moved it from this house," Ivan said. "Maybe there's nothing here."

"Maybe," he said. Then as we sat on the couch in the living room it dawned on me. "What about the attic?"

We looked for a flashlight, went up to check it and found nothing. "Well, we tried," I said. "You want anything out of here? I saw a few pieces of jewelry on the dresser."

We walked back into the room and he began to look through his jewelry box. Ivan picked up a chain and a Rolex. "I'll rock these."

"No, you'll need to sell them," I said as I plopped back onto the bed that I'd first fucked Jermaine in. "If you get caught wearing any of that stuff by anyone who knew him, it wouldn't be good for you."

"Nia, you are something else."

I smiled and in the excitement of the moment I pulled him onto the bed and kissed him. The kisses sent quick sparks through my body and my animal instincts kicked in. "Let's fuck."

Ivan looked over at me and I saw from the look on his face that he wanted me too. He couldn't be around me without getting a hard on. I loved it. I stood up and slid my jeans off. "Are you serious? We gotta get out here."

"Come on."

Sensing that I was dead serious, he put the watch on his wrist and eased closer to me. I unzipped his pants and pulled his meat out. I took him in my mouth and felt him growing. As the head began to hit the back of my throat he began to breathe heavier. "I love the way you suck my dick, Nia."

I hit him off as if I was trying to suck the secret to the universe out of him. I cupped his balls and massaged them as I tongued the underside of his dick. Up and down, I went as I panted and slurped.

"Fuck me, now," I said.

"Let me eat you first."

I begged him to give me what I wanted but he had his way, pushing my legs back to my face and diving in. He licked me long enough to get me wet, then he flipped me over and pulled me onto my knees. I prepared for him to enter me doggie-style. But instead of the tip of his penis, I got more tongue. He started licking my slit from the back, then he moved up to my asshole and started licking the rim as if it were a sundae. It tickled, but turned me on at the same time. In my book there was nothing nastier than eating someone's ass, and that got me off.

His saliva was running down my crack onto the bed as he penetrated the opening to my anus, lips locked on the hole, tongue a half inch deep. I started to rub my pussy while the side of my face was being smashed into the mattress. I stared at the fish in Jermaine's tank, gliding through the water as I glided towards an orgasm.

I was about to come when he pulled his mouth away. "Shit," I said quietly at first. Then I yelled, "Ohhhh, shit," loudly. "What... are... you... doing?" He was smashing the head of his dick into my asshole.

He gripped my cheeks and my hole went 'POP' as the head made its way through. I was soaked, so his dick slid in as if it belonged there. He didn't take it slow. He moved fast as if he was scared that I'd make him stop. But I wasn't. If he liked it, I loved it. I began to hump him back. "You want this ass?" I moaned.

"Yeah... I ... ahhhh," he was feeling immense pleasure.

"Then fuck it, motherfucker. Fuck my ass," I said.

We started a battle. He stroked me deep and I eased back on to his dick making him feel as if I was fucking him.

I'd tried anal with Ali, some time back but had never got into it. Maybe, Ali was too big, but Ivan was perfect. Together we created a rhythm and heat that had us both racing toward a climax. I jammed three fingers in my pussy as he started to pound my ass like a mad man.

"Yeahhhhh," he screamed. "I'm about to come in your ass."

"Come for me, baby. Shoot it all up in this ass."

"Ahhhhhhhhhhhhh," he said as he began to empty his nut into my bowels. I felt the warmth and I exploded.

"Ohhhhhh, yesssss, Ivan.... Yes, yes, fuck.... Uhhhhhhh," I came hard and jumped forward off of his dick as my legs trembled uncontrollably.

He collapsed and tried to catch his breath on the bed next to me.

After laying still and relaxing while staring at the sharks swimming gracefully about, an idea came to my mind. I got up and walked over to the tank. I stuck my arm down into the water, into the gravel and started to move it out the way. I felt plastic underneath it.

"What are you doing?" he asked as I took the net and captured the sharks one by one. I dropped them both into the toilet. I left the bedroom and came back after grabbing a baseball bat that I'd noticed earlier in the corner of the basement. Gripping the bat like Barry Bonds, I swung with all my might, crushing the glass on my first swing, sending gallons of water pouring onto the floor.

Ivan jumped up to see that the custom made fish tank had a bottom that went much deeper that you could see with it buried in the wall. I scooped the gravel away and revealed packages of shrink-wrapped money, stacked neatly in the bottom of the tank.

"I'll be damned," he said. "Ain't that some shit."

I nodded believing that maybe I had indeed sucked the secret of the universe right out of his dick or that maybe he'd fucked it out of my ass.

Be Waiting for You

Chapter 19

I tried to be a fair person. I tried to do what I thought was fair. I had Ivan deliver one hundred and fifty thousand dollars to Big Lenny. At least that was the plan. When I called Big Lenny to tie up our loose ends, he went off and he had good reason to. Ivan never showed up.

Ivan and I had gone back to my apartment and spent two days counting seven hundred and forty thousand dollars. I gave him twenty percent, one hundred and forty-eight grand. A nice hit for a college drop-out. That was enough for him to get the Jaguar that he'd lied about having when we met and to actually open a studio of his own, instead of renting hours.

Instead of thanking me, he fucked me one last time. He decided to keep Big Lenny's twenty percent and then he did what anyone in his position would do. He vanished.

"I'm going to kill you, Jayla. You fucked me. You fucked Big Lenny."

"Listen, I didn't do anything, but…"

His voice was like a mad scientist. He wasn't making any sense of what I was saying. "Why would I have even told you that I went and got the money, Lenny?"

"I don't know. You're fucking with my head, bitch. You done fucked over the wrong one."

He kept insisting that I had found millions and didn't want to give him any of it. "Lenny, I'll tell you what," I said. "I'll give you a hundred grand…"

"Fuck that. I know where you're from. I want my share or I'll go and kill your mama, or that bitch who used to dance here with you. You'll see…"

I hung up on him. He'd lost his mind and to be honest, the wannabe commando scared me. It didn't matter if I gave him every cent, the nigga was going to come after me. It took me a day to pack up my belongings, the furniture I'd have to leave. The next morning, I drove to the Marriot Hotel out near Hartsfield International Airport and got three rooms. I stuffed all the money that would fit into the safes and put the rest in the trunk of my car underneath the spare.

It took me half a day riding around in pouring rain, to find a rental car place that would let me get a car without a credit card. I wound up having to drop a hundred dollar tip and promise a date to the country ass manager at Budget, in order to let me drive off the lot in the LeSabre.

I didn't care how many copies he had made of my fake I.D., he would never see the car again. After leaving there, I drove the car to a shop in Decatur that paid cash for airbags and waited twenty minutes while they took them out of the steering wheel and passenger's seat. Next, I stopped off at the AutoZone and bought two five gallon gas tanks, filled them up and headed toward the club.

At twelve midnight I let the air out of one of the tires on Big Lenny's Suburban and climbed back into the rental car that I'd parked in the rear of the lot. The club closed at one A.M. since it was Wednesday night. As usual Big Lenny escorted the last of the girls to their cars and went back in to tell Polo he was leaving. Polo usually spent another couple of hours in his office. He wasn't afraid of being left by himself. Since Polo walked around with bigger guns than Dirty Harry he felt completely secure.

Big Lenny walked out the door as I watched. He finally noticed that his tire was flat and I could see from the way his body moved that he was cursing. He looked at his watch and reached into the back of his truck to gather his jack.

I picked up my phone and called the car service, "Yes, I'll need a cab." I gave them the address for the motel that was two blocks up. "Tell the driver to wait if I'm not right out, I'll pay extra. Thanks."

I watched him pull the spare off the back of his vehicle. It took him less than five minutes to get the lugs off and lift his truck into the air. Then he squatted down as he lined the holes in the rim up with the lug. As he spun the bolts on, he had no clue that I had circled the lot and was now barreling toward him at thirty miles an hour.

My heart was beating like a bomb with every beat. Big Lenny never knew what hit him as he was crushed and pinned between the two vehicles. I didn't even want to look to see if he was dead or alive, I didn't have the time. Instead, I hopped out of the car with the stocking on my face and my baseball cap pulled low. I took the knobs off both containers of gas, tipped them over, and then squirted the lighter fluid on the wheel and the seat I'd just gotten out of.

I couldn't run fast enough once I tossed the match into the seat. The flames shot up like a fountain. By the time I reached the street the explosions started. I hated that Ivan's actions put me in that predicament and that Lenny's threats had forced me to do that.

When I got to the motel a couple blocks up from the club the cab was waiting on me. He dropped me off at the airport and from there, I hopped another cab to the hotel. I ran a bubble bath and drank a half bottle of wine.

I slept unbelievably sound. Maybe it was the fact that I knew my life was about to start over. A new chapter was on the horizon. Even if it was going to be rough, I was ready. In the morning I was going home. I knew that legal fees were high, but with nearly a half a million dollars I was prepared to fight any charges against me.

I knew that it was ironic that I'd run, hid, robbed and now killed just to get my life back.

The conversation that I had with myself on the way to D.C. was a long and deep one.

Every mile and every minute of my trip found me dissecting episode after episode of my recent experiences. The tears seemed to pour out of my face from Charlotte to Raleigh. The anger bubbled up in me to the point where I wanted to destroy something for the next couple of hours after that. By the time I reached Northern Virginia, the only emotion that I could wrap myself around was sadness.

As I crossed the Woodrow Wilson bridge reaching Maryland, for the first time I understood that I was depressed. I was sick and I'd been like that since the day my father left me. What happened to my family was equal to me catching a disease that seemed impossible to recover from. The violence that came from the deceit practiced by my mother had set the tone for the destructive path that I'd traveled down for the past five years.

I'd had a long drive to plan my upcoming moves and when pulled up to the self-storage office on Allentown Road I already knew exactly what I was going to say.

"I'd like to pay for this storage bin for the next two years. I'm traveling to Africa with the Peace Corps and I need to keep my furniture stored. Can I pay for it that far in advance?"

"We love customers who do things like that," the portly woman replied.

"I'll be back in the morning with my furniture. Thanks." I received my code and my key and left.

When the next day arrived, I had the furniture I'd purchased from the second hand store delivered by the owner and his son. They hadn't had a sale like mine in years and were glad to bring it over for me. I'd taken a mismatch couch and loveseat, a raggedy old, bedroom suite, a lumpy mattress, assorted lamps and a baby crib.

In accordance with my plan, I went out to the Value City and bought a complete carload of things that would clutter up the storage bin. After I unloaded it all, I carefully hid four hundred thousand dollars inside some of the various items.

After a short nap I took a shower and checked out of the Comfort Inn, with a trunk full of clothes and forty thousand dollars in my handbag. I rode around for a while taking in the city trying to decide what to do to pass the time. Since the March weather in D.C. was worse than the dead of winter in Atlanta, I found myself in Nordstrom out in Crystal City, looking for a coat.

Needing to pass some more time, I went and got my nails and feet done. Finally at five, I headed back toward my destination. I pulled off the Beltway and headed up Route 202 until I reached Lake Arbor Way. I made the first turn and drove around the winding road until I reached my mother and Dean's house.

The front door was open inside the storm door. As I parked my car one house away, I saw my mother was carrying grocery bags into the house. She'd put on a couple of pounds, but was still as beautiful as ever. I fought back the tears and sat still. *How could I even greet her? How could I face her after everything I'd done, after the monster I'd become?*

I took a deep breath and pulled up behind her car. She closed her trunk and looked back at me. I watched as she dropped the grocery bags to the ground and ran toward me.

I barely made it out of the door before she clenched me by both shoulders, "Baby, is that... ohmilord...and savior," she grabbed me. "Nia, oh, my baby." I didn't say a word as we embraced one another. She kept saying, "Nia, Nia... my baby."

The only thing I could think of to say was, "Mama, I'm so sorry," the tears began to fall. She grabbed the stuff from the ground and whisked me into the house.

"I've missed you so much. Are you okay?"

"Yeah, I've missed you too, mama."

"Listen to you, with your country accent. Where have you been, down south?"

"Yeah," I said.

"I knew it. I felt it. I had dreams. I'd see you. I knew you weren't up north." She kept hugging me. "I can't believe how good you look. You're a grown woman... you... grew....up on me. You're driving a Mercedes?"

I nodded.

"My baby... I... can't believe it's you," she said and then burst into tears. It was so emotional. We both cried for the next twenty minutes off and on. I finally suggested that she pour us a glass of wine to help us calm our nerves.

"That's a good idea," she said. It worked. We were able to talk for the next twenty minutes without losing it. She took me downstairs and when I saw my room still intact, I couldn't believe it. I've kept it for you, all this time. Of course, I updated the bedding and curtains, but I wanted it here for you whenever you came home."

No sooner than she mentioned coming home I heard Dean walk through the door. "Whose car is that in the driveway?" he yelled.

When I appeared at the top of the steps with my mother his face was frozen, "Nia?"

I nodded. He took me off guard, hugging me as if I were *his* daughter. During the embrace I tried to muster up some hatred for him, but I couldn't. I had learned so much about life and what passion made people do that I almost understood his connection with my mother. Right or wrong, people were drawn to one another. Sometimes they stayed together, sometimes it all fell apart. I'd lived it and now I understood.

I spent the next hour telling the two of them sketchy details and lies about my life in Atlanta. "Nia, anything you need, you have," Dean said. "We've missed you. Your mother has been through hell, without you. Not knowing if you were okay..." now he was choked up. "We were always so happy when the postcards came. They always came just when your mother seemed on the verge of a breakdown. I did my best to make her feel better, but without you, she was always incomplete. Thank GOD, you're home, Nia,"

Oddly, I was touched. He really loved my mother. It was apparent. He was however, a businessman by nature and he didn't waste time getting down to the pressing issue. "There are some things you might need to address, you're going to need help, and I have a lawyer on retainer."

It was then that my mother explained that there had in fact been a warrant for me. It wasn't for my arrest, but rather I was wanted as a material witness in Tony's shooting. "It's been so long and as I understand the boy, Ali, has been convicted already."

Hearing his name sent a pang of gloom through my body. "Yeah, I guess I'll find out."

I spent the entire weekend with my mother. I wasn't ready to start visiting family and extended family, so I begged her to keep my return under wraps for the time being. I agreed with Dean and wanted to focus on my possible issues with the law.

On Monday, I met with Dean's attorney, a stunning dynamo of a woman named Heather Pinkney. By the time I'd arrived at her office down on Indiana Avenue, Miss Pinkney had already researched my case. I was amazed that she didn't look a day over twenty five, yet she was so sharp. Beautiful chocolate skin, lovely locks and a voice that sounded inviting, yet authoritative. She told me a little about her background. I was amazed to hear that she'd grown up in Southeast, just like me, and yet she'd taken a different road, which was why she was sitting on the opposite side of the desk from me. Seeing and talking with her inspired me that I could still become something good one day. Maybe, I'd be in a position to help a young girl find her way one day.

Sitting across from her on the Victorian-styled chairs, she broke it all down for me. "Nia, your situation is good and bad. The good news is that the warrant for you has expired, in respect to the case in which you were wanted for questioning has already been tried. I'll say that it's a good thing for you that Ali was convicted.

The bad news is that you may have to eventually answer some questions about your flight. The best advice I can give you should that come about is to give a statement regarding your leaving under duress."

"Duress?"

"Pressure, fear from Ali. This could bring about more charges for Ali, but in his case it doesn't really matter. He's never getting out of jail. I did look over his testimony and never did he mention your name. He cited no motive for killing Tony than self-defense."

"So, what do I do now? Do I have to turn myself in?"

"I'll see if I can get the prosecutor to strike the warrant. They may have simply forgotten to do it when the trial was over. If they do it, then you're pretty much in the clear. If not, then that means they'll want to talk to you. At that point, I'll step in and take the necessary steps."

"So is there any chance that I could go to jail?"

"For any involvement in this? I doubt it." She paused and said, "Now, there is the murder of a Shante Grayson, who was a witness for the prosecution, that went unsolved. The prosecutor was unable to pin that on Ali and believe me, they desperately wanted to, but he had an alibi. The detective who was on that case retired a year and a half back. At the time he believed that Ali was guilty of that too, so when he got the conviction and the life sentence it seemed to satisfy the District of Columbia."

"So that means?"

"It means that you aren't charged with it and unless, you did it, were seen by someone doing it who hasn't come forward, or she comes back from the grave to say you did it, it won't be an issue."

"I didn't do it."

"Then, I think… everything is gonna work out for you. I'm in tomorrow and Wednesday, but I'll let you know something by Friday at the latest."

I walked out of her office feeling optimistic, thankful, yet still a little scared. Until there was no chance at all of my going to jail for this, I wouldn't rest easy. For some reason, I didn't have any fears about being caught for what I did to Big Lenny.

They say when you commit a murder you make a thousand and one errors. I thought about the I.D. I'd given the rental car manager. How he never once looked at the picture of the Hispanic woman because he'd focused on my tits, which were purposely hanging out of my shirt the entire time I was there.

I was careful that they didn't have a camera system in there. I'd walked out of two places earlier. I'd switched wigs in each cab, as well as accents. If I'd made a thousand and one mistakes, I was confident that I'd burned up a thousand of them.

"Fuck Lenny," I said as I drove home.

Destiny's Children
Chapter 20

Whoever said you couldn't go home again didn't tell a lie. It was like trying to fit a square peg into a round hole. Three months had passed and I was starting to get bored out of my mind. I actually missed Atlanta. I missed reducing men to defenseless mush while I danced on the stage. It wasn't so much that I loved stripping, it was more of the fact that I missed the action.

When the summer rolled around, I was actually a legitimate citizen, driving a car that was in my name, with insurance and everything. I'd gotten a real driver's license a week after Heather had cleared up my legal problems. Things were going well for me on a few fronts but I was still bored. I had no plan and no where to go.

On Father's Day weekend, I'd decided to take the three hour ride to go and visit my old man on Saturday. The ride was relaxing but seeing my father after all these years was the most gut wrenching experience of my life. The second the door buzzed and he walked into the visiting room, the despair took a temporary hold on me. I knew that I might never see him outside of these walls again.

He held me and we both cried for several minutes before trying to find the words to open up to one other. Finally, I just started by confessing to my father everything that I'd been through. From the stripping, to the sex, to the murders. He didn't seem surprised.

I told him nearly every single, sordid, detail of my life, except for the money I'd come into. I knew he'd want to spend it on a lawyer trying to get his sentence overturned. But he'd killed a state trooper. Even I knew that he was lucky that he wasn't on death row.

He cried like a baby as we hugged again after my confession. "I thought you didn't love me anymore. All this time, I never knew what you were going through so much."

"I'll always love you, daddy. No matter what," I wiped the snot from my nose. "For the rest of your life, you won't have to want for anything. I'll make sure you have whatever they allow."

He shook his head in disbelief. "My little angel. God told me that you were coming. He told an angel was coming."

We spent the afternoon catching up. He shared his spiritual development and urged me to build a relationship with Christ. I told him that I was bored now that I was home. "Who says you have to stay home? Home is where the heart is. See the world. Be what you want to be?"

I smiled at him. I let him in on the fact that I wasn't sure what else I wanted to do other than make a bunch of money. "Well, then go get paid. Find out how to make some money and hold onto it. The information is out there but they hiding from black folks."

"Hiding it?"

"Yeah, they keep all the valuable information the last place where we're going to look, in books."

I laughed and thought about what he'd said. I admitted that I hadn't read a book in a good while. "I'll send you a few of mine that I want you to read."

I was about to leave when he said, "Hey, I have a partner I want you to meet." He stood up and yelled over. "Hey, New York, come here. I want you to meet my daughter."

I looked up and saw a tall handsome man walk over to us. He'd been sitting with his family. His sister and his mother had come down to visit him, bringing his son.

He stopped at our table and the sight of him took my breath away. "New York, this my daughter, Nia," my father said proudly.

"Nice to meet you," I said.

"The pleasure is all mine," he said. "Your father has always talked about you. From the day I met him. It's good to put a face to the person," he said. "Also, you can call me Trey."

"I'm going to give you Trey's information. Maybe you could write him. He's a good kid," My father said. "He caught a bad break, but when he gets out of here, he's going straight to the top."

"The top?" I asked.

"I rap. I'm a rapper. I was about to get signed to Def Jam before I caught a charge down here, but I'll be out in a couple of years. Maybe less."

"Yeah, New York is the same age as you, twenty-one," my father said.

I laughed, "Next month, I'll be twenty-one next month."

"Well, I'd love to hear from you, but I understand that a beautiful young lady like yourself might not have the time."

"We'll have to see," I said.

We shook hands but I really wanted give his ass a hug. The nigga walked off in those bland khakis and no-name polo shirt as if he were in a three-thousand dollar suit. He moved like a king.

"That boy is going to do something with himself. Mark my words," my father said.

"How do you know him?"

"When he got here, a few young cats from southeast were trying to move on him. He was a lone outsider. But I felt his energy. He was a good cat, but he wasn't going to back down. They were going to kill him. I intervened and he's been like a son to me since."

"That's nice, but you be careful," I said.

"Don't worry about me."

We ended the visit and I tried not to cry as I left the prison. It was strange but even with him being locked up, seeing my father made me feel whole again. I couldn't wait to go shopping for him. I might even pick up a couple things for New York. Thinking about that damned New York had my juices flowing. I tried to shake it off and charge it to the fact that I'd been out of action for a minute.

On Sunday, my mother had a cookout. I felt horrible when I saw Julia for the first time. I had gotten used to the crying every time I saw someone who I'd known for years. But seeing her was different, because I felt sorry for her. She'd lost her son-slash-daughter. I would never tell her what I knew about it. She told me the version that she believed and I consoled her as best I could.

When Harold showed up, I had a mix of emotions. He had his three year-old daughter with him. She looked like a piece of heaven if I ever saw it. She had light brown, curly, hair. It hung down to her shoulders. She was dressed in a Baby Phat outfit and pink Air Jordans. I couldn't believe how much she looked like both he and Brandy.

"What took you so long to let somebody see your ass?" He asked as he approached.

"Don't start with me, man. I've been trying to keep it together. One day at a time."

"Okay, alright. You get a pass this time."

He and I hugged until I couldn't breathe. "So where is Brandy?" I asked.

"We're not together anymore. Didn't your mother tell you?"

"Tell me what?"

"I caught her with another woman. She said that she was in love, so I told her to do her thang but that Nia wasn't going to grow up around that."

"Nia?"

"Yeah, we named her after you," he laughed and wrapped his hand around my shoulder. "But, fuck her. Let's me and you go catch up. I missed your crazy ass."

We spent the day playing with Nia in the pool. I couldn't believe they'd named her after me. I felt so honored.

As the sun began to set, Harold asked me, "So cousin, what are you going to do with yourself."

That was a good ass question. One that I didn't have the answer to. I asked him what DeMarcus was doing these days.

"He goes to the University of Maryland. He's into riding motorcycles. Not much else."

"He have a girlfriend?"

"Yeah, last I talked to him. We don't hang like we used to. I'm a single father so I don't have time to party and I damned sure ain't riding a motorcycle."

My cousin had matured so much while I was gone. He had me feeling like Rip Van Winkle. I felt bad about Brandy and I wondered if he'd been hurt by her. I even wondered if she was hurting.

The next day I woke up trying to figure out what I'd do with the rest of my life. I decided to do some research, see if I could find something that I wanted to do. I walked downstairs into my mother's office and logged on to the Internet.

I'd never really searched it before, so when I started typing in things and seeing information pop up, I was amazed. I typed in my own name and my old address popped up, which was scary.

Next I typed in Ali's name and some articles about his case popped up. When I went to the Bureau of Prisons website and typed in his DIN number the name of the correctional facility and the directions came up. I thought about visiting him, but then Big Lenny's words came back to me along with some of the pain.

I was about look for a GED course when I thought about one more person I wanted to find. For the hell of it, I typed in Ivan's name. A D.C. address popped up and a phone number. I couldn't believe it. I stepped away and grabbed the phone and dialed the number.

"Hello," a woman answered the phone.

"Yes, this is a friend of Ivan's. Is he there?"

"He just ran to the store, but he'll be right back. Who's calling?"

I hung up.

Even though I had every reason in the world to let it go, I picked up the phone and started looking for rental cars.

. . . four years later @
The Kodak Theater, Hollywood, California
2004 BET AWARDS

I couldn't believe one of the celebrities had the nerve to come out of her mouth disrespectfully. "I wonder who those bitches had to fuck to get these seats?" she asked as we walked past.

I wasn't sure who'd said it, but when I looked back I saw, Meagan Goode, Lisa Raye and Vivica Fox all seated behind us. Destiny was ready to fight but I laughed and pulled her by the arm. We were in the same Cavalli, Armani and Dior dresses that they wore, the same eight hundred dollar shoes and rocked the same ice in our ears as they did. The only difference was, we had better seats than a bunch of black, A-list, actors, singers and rappers and it was killing them because they didn't know who we were.

"Don't pay that shit no mind," I said. "This is Hollywood, if a bitch ain't hating on you, you ain't doin' shit." We kept walking until we reached the fifth row. I stopped at the end of the row and let Destiny and Brandy walk in and take their seats first.

I could hear the voices around me saying, "Mmmmph, look at her."

One of the guys from G-Unit said, "I'll see you after the show baby."

Indeed they would. I would be heading to at least three after parties.

As we watched Kanye perform *Jesus Walks* I looked over at Brandy, who was completely enamored with the dancing.

She could emulate Beyonce, and most of the hottest R&B artist who were good dancers, Mya and Ciara included. I knew she'd make it as a dancer and fulfill her dreams of being recognized for something that she was passionate about. She'd been working so hard at her dancing that she had actually earned a try-out to become a Heat Dancer. If she made it Harold had agreed to move to Miami with her. He was in love with her and his daughter.

She and Harold had gotten back together once she'd been honest with him about her ambiguous sexual taste. Once he accepted that she was bisexual, and stopped judging her, she lost her desire to constantly sleep with women and came home to him. The wilding out became an every now and then thing for her. To my surprise, Harold admitted to me that he enjoyed bringing another woman into the bedroom with them every now and again.

Destiny and I moved to New York together and got an apartment off of Ninth Avenue in Manhattan. She enrolled in school at the Fashion Institute of Technology and got a job at Scores on the West Side to keep the money rolling in until she finished. She was even looking for a space to open up another Laundromat in the city.

I'd long grown tired of dancing and decided to set a goal. I wanted to make a couple million dollars any way I could as long as it was legal. Then I wanted to settle down, have a couple of kids and to one day up open my front door for the cameras of MTV Cribs. Even after the life I'd lived I still believed that happily ever after was possible.

Taking my father's advice, I'd started reading a bunch of books and came across something interesting in one of the ones he turned me onto called *The Come Up Chronicles*. It was based on a true story about three women who used their looks, bodies and brains in a race to get rich. He'd told me that

I could wind up like any one of the girls in the book, making smart decisions would determine which one. My inspiration came from one of the characters in the book who said that the quickest way to come into money was to hang around people who had plenty of it.

After Usher won the award for the best male artist we prepared to make our exit. I knew that Ivan was going be in a great mood. He'd worked on one of the tracks on his album. I was happy for him. I was happy for me. More people would want to work with him, bringing more money into I-Rock Studios, a studio that I owned half of.

In exchange for me not killing him, or making his life complete hell, Ivan and I became partners and opened the studio in downtown Atlanta. I never trusted him again, and had every thing set up through an attorney. Heather had hooked me up with an entertainment lawyer who specialized in keeping crooks honest with each other. It turned out to be a great move.

After having blown through most of the four hundred thousand I'd gotten from Jermaine, I lived decent on the hundred grand a year that I made from I-Rock, but was still determined to see some *real* money.

I also had done a few photo shoots for hip-hop magazines, been eye-candy, done back-shots and been a smooth girl. But it wasn't until the man my father called New York came home that I agreed to appear in a music video.

My father hadn't lied about his talent. He'd been home for a year and the streets were buzzing with word about his new album. He was going to be the hottest thing in the rap world since Jay-Z, who had retired. People were hating on 50, and Nas didn't seem to want to take the throne, so there was a void in the birthplace of Hip-hop.

Between sets my phone rang. It was Ivan. "Where ya'll at?"

"We about to leave and head to the party," I said.

"Alright there's some one here who you need to meet. He's seen your pictures and he wants you in his video." Ivan had passed on the awards show, said he was tired of the fanfare and the red carpet after going to the past three.

"You know how I feel about doing music videos. That's not my thing. I only did Trey's because... well you know why."

"When it airs next week and is the number one video on BET and MTV, everybody is going to want you. So you might as well be ready."

"Ready for what?"

"Your life is going to change."

"I hear you. I'll check you in a bit."

As I followed Trey out of the Kodak Theater, I watched him move through the crowd with the same confident walk he'd had in that visiting room four years ago.

We'd formed a bond during the couple of years that he finished up his sentence. I'd sent him letters, pictures and whatever else he wanted. We didn't try to start a relationship while he was in. He was too smart for that; didn't want me to disappoint him while he was inside and he didn't want to disappoint me when he got out. He opted for the love without the romance. It was a smart choice for both of us.

He didn't know it, but I had deep feelings for him, though I wouldn't let it get in the way of our friendship. I needed him in my life and I was willing to fight the overwhelming desires to be wifey. I knew trying to force a relationship would be the surest way to lose what we shared.

We made it through crowd out into the lobby and photographers and fans spotted us.

"Hey, Trey."

"What's good, Trey."

"Yo, there's Trey G."

"Get a picture."

He was a star, on the verge of becoming *the* star of stars.

The khaki's were long gone now as he was rocking a hundred-thousand dollars worth of clothing and jewelry.

Because all eyes were on him, all eyes were on me.

I heard someone say, "Isn't that Nia Morgan. The chick from the magazine?"

Beaming with pride at being recognized I realized then that this was all a set up for what was coming next.

Stay tuned for
The King of New York

For Discussion:

1. What impact do you think Nia's father's going to jail had on the path she went down?

2. Is not having a father figure ever an excuse for a girl to go completely wild?

3. Do you think that people inherit violent tempers? Do you think it was Nia's environment that caused her to act so violently or was she repeatedly thrust into 'survive or perish' situations?

4. What type of issues do you think the author challenges the reader to examine in reading this book, if anything?

5. Ultimately was Nia smart or lucky? Did she surprise you with her actions at all?

6. Do you feel the author wrote the novel with a particular audience in mind? Who else could identify with this novel? Would you recommend it to anyone?

7. Nia was really down for her friends, seemingly with no limits as to what she'd do to protect them? Is this realistic?

8. This book was very sexual? Do you think that sex was used *too* much to tell the story?

9. How much of an effect do you feel Nia's use of drugs had on her losing control of her life?

10. Where would a guy like Ali get his development from, how would he come to be how he was? Who was your favorite character? Least favorite?

11. When Brandy came on to Nia do you think she was more vulnerable, curious or simply horny?

12. Nia and DeMarcus never seemed to *get* one another. How different were they?

13. Is it possible for a person to bounce back from the things that Nia went through?

14. Which character, if any, do you most relate to? How do you believe that the tendencies of these characters reflect things that are in you?

15. How significant was Nia's going to see her father?

16. Should Nia be considered a leader or a follower? Good or Evil?

19. Did you have a favorite part of the book? A least favorite?

20. This book was a prequel to another book, The King of New York. How do you imagine Nia will play into that? Do you plan on reading it?

Nvision Publishing Order Form

Brand New   **Brand New**   **Brand New**

st Lane by
one Williams

A Taste of Honey
Darren Coleman

Add $4.25 for shipping
Priority Mail. Total of 19.25
for orders being shipped di
prisons Nvision Publishing
25%. Cost are as follows, $1
shipping for a total of $15.50.

Make money order pa
Nvision Publishing. Only cer
government issued checks.

No PERSONAL CHECKS

Send to:
Nvision Publishing/Order P.O. Box 274
Lanham Severn Road, Lanham, MD 20703

Purchaser Information - Name

_____

Register #_____ (Applies if incarcerated)

Address_____

City_____   **State/Zip**_____

Which Books_____

# of books_____   **Total enclosed $**_____

Life Changing Books Order Form

Add $4.25 for shipping via U.S. Priority Mail. Total of 19.25 per book for orders being shipped directly to prisons Nvision Publishing deducts 25%. <u>Cost are as follows,</u> $11.25 plus shipping for a total of $15.45.

Make money order payable to <u>Life Changing Books</u>. Only certified or government issued checks.

Send to:
Life Changing Books/Orders P.O. Box 423
Brandywine, MD 20613

Purchaser Information

Name_____

Register #_____
        (Applies if incarcerated)

Address_____

City_____ State/Zip_____

Which Books_____

# of books_____ Total enclosed $_____

Over 20 titles available. Order one of these and request a catalogue.

DARREN COLEMAN
the Don of Urban Fiction

A TASTE OF HONEY

As the writer it's hard for me to say that one piece of my
rk is greater than the others. I have to let the fans decide, but
jump out there and say that *A Taste of Honey* has to be up
re. You may like the overt sexiness of this book, *Get Low,* or
1 may prefer the grittiness and action in *Do or Die.* A lot of
1 will love the honesty and insight of the characters in *Before*
et Go best of all, but I will tell you why you should run out
l cop *A Taste of Honey.*

I worked really hard to make it a grown and sexy literary
perience. I traveled to the places I talked about in the book,
ked with people who lived the lives of the characters and even
dressed some of my own demons through the story, all the
ile blowing a deadline to ensure that the book was right.

It is my mission to write books that are unpredictable and
A Taste of Honey you will surely be kept guessing up to the
t minute as to how the story will turn out.

It's got plenty of edge, with a romantic twist, on top of a
pense-filled plot. If you've enjoyed any of my work, or if
1 are a new reader – *A Taste of Honey* is a must read!

Be sure to let me know how you liked it. Send me a
nd request at www.myspace.com/darrencolemanbooks.

**Available wherever you buy books
and @ Amazon.com**

Essence BESTSELLING AUTHOR OF *Before I Let Go* AND *Don't Ever Wonder*

DARREN COLEMAN

A NOVEL

A TASTE of HONEY

Some women won't stop until they get what they want ...